THE MATRIARCH
AND
THE MAGIC

To Grace
and Jadyn-
Welcome to Irth!
What's your magic!
Yours in writing

Nan Whybark
March 2013

THE MATRIARCH AND THE MAGIC

BOOK 3 OF THE EARTH TO IRTH SERIES

Nan Whybark

iUniverse, Inc.
Bloomington

THE MATRIARCH AND THE MAGIC
BOOK 3 OF THE EARTH TO IRTH SERIES

iUniverse books may be ordered through booksellers or by contacting:

iUniverse
1663 Liberty Drive
Bloomington, IN 47403
www.iuniverse.com
1-800-Authors (1-800-288-4677)

ISBN: 978-1-4759-7369-3 (sc)
ISBN: 978-1-4759-7404-1 (hc)
ISBN: 978-1-4759-7370-9 (ebk)

Library of Congress Control Number: 2013901868

Printed in the United States of America

iUniverse rev. date: 02/07/2013

Dedicated to
Frances Lenore Decker Newby,
my mother
and high matriarch,
who taught me about courage to the end.

IRTH'S GLOSSARY FOR OFF-WORLDERS

am'Oran: A series of large underwater caverns which form the communities of this city populated by the am'Orans.

am'Orans: A race of gentle humanoids who are child-like in their appearance with pale-blue skin, large dark-blue eyes, and white hair. They live in underwater cave communities. They have gill vents on their necks for underwater breathing, and also lungs to breathe air. They have established trade with land dwellers on Irth. Their trade items include shining shells, delicate deep-sea fish, singing sea turtles and other rarities from the sea.

am'Oranth: The early rising first moon of Irth. It has a soft pearly-white luster which is dim, yet beautiful. It is said the am'Oran people were named for this moon due to their pale, luminous complexions (Also see ul'Daman, Irth's other moon).

AquaVelvet Fish: A blue-green fish which has velvety skin highly prized for making exotic hats and bags. Also good to eat with squirting sea plums and muffybread.

Birth-gift: A magical ability which is inherited at birth by those of Irth. The gift is not evident at first, but usually surfaces in children by the age of four or five. The children must then learn to use, control and strengthen their gift as they grow to maturity. Parents and schools help in this process. Some gifts may determine future jobs or duties.

Bloat Fish: A smallish, tan-colored fish which has an inner sac it inflates with air to make itself too large to be swallowed by an attacking predator (also see Waterblimp).

Bottom Spider: An eight-legged crustacean about eight inches long with two body parts. They are edible, although their meat is very salty and mushy. They are helpful in cleaning up debris on the sea floor. They are food for many types of fish and other creatures.

Breakfast bug: A tiny insect which often flies blindly into spider webs, containers of food or drink in the early light of morning. Hence it is often eaten for breakfast intentionally or accidentally. High in protein and other nutrients, it is largely ignored or even considered good fortune when found in something about to be eaten.

Bumphead: A pasture animal the size of a huge dog. It has long, shaggy hair, horns which grow down and forward from the sides of the head just under the tiny, upright ears, and dark pink eyes with triangular pupils. It is usually a gentle animal, but during mating season the male becomes violent, ramming into other males with its head. This ramming behavior often creates permanent lumps on the head. The bumpier the head, the stronger the animal is thought to be. Often the extending horns cause damage to their heads and faces as well. It is bred primarily in Leppash and highly prized for the female's sweetwater, male's horns used in making tools and instruments, and hair used in creating yarn for weaving fabrics. Its hair is silky soft and usually off white or, very rarely, emerald-green. These rarities are reserved only for the patriarchal family and the extremely wealthy. They are considered good luck and are never killed for meat or sport, but their hair is sheared and sold yearly (see also Sweetwater).

City Council Representative: A member of the High Council, this person's main duty is to represent the voice of the common people of en'Edlia on matters discussed at council meetings. He or she must be impartial to their own desires and vote as the majority of the people dictate. The representative also brings to the council items of concern brought up in city council meetings, and then returns the High Council decisions or suggestions on those matters to the city council. Birth-gifts which help in this position are all-hearing ears and mental-audio memory. Currently Patriarch Pepperton holds this position.

Crown Matriarch: If there is no son born to the ruling family, the eldest daughter becomes crown matriarch at her father's death. If the high matriarch is still living, she and the crown matriarch take on a co-leadership position until the high matriarch's death. At which time, the crown matriarch becomes high matriarch and her husband, if she has one, takes up the title of high patriarch.

Crown Patriarch: The eldest son of a high patriarch, who usually inherits the title of high patriarch at his father's death. In some cases, the husband of a crown matriarch would be considered crown patriarch until the high matriarch's death. Then he would assume the position of high patriarch (see Crown Matriarch).

Dark Magic: The evil side of magic, avoided by most on Irth, but embraced by those seeking power, riches, or other undue glory and desiring to take it by force. Such was the magic of the Wizard Zarcon (see Book 1—"The Weasel and the Wizard") and the Sorceress Odethia (see Book 2—"The Serpent and the Sorceress").

Dragon's Landing: An eastern seaside city in the country of en'Edlia (see map). It is a lesser trade port frequented by dragon riders, dragon raisers, egg traders, and those with similar interests.

en'Edlia: The largest country on Irth, ruled by a patriarchal/council system. It is a major seaport and trade center. The royal crest is a white and gold winged seashell on a field of emerald-green. Current high patriarch is Merrickobrokt, son of Broktomerris and Narrianamyesa.

et'Altere: A group of villages under one ruler, The Great Altere, in the Altere Mountains (see et'Alterens; Great Altere; also map)

et'Alterens: The people from the et'Altere villages who often dress in furs of animals for warmth. They are called et'Als as slang for et'Alterens by some people of larger cities and are somewhat looked down upon as less educated and cultured. This is not true, but a perceived notion due to the shy and reclusive nature of these people. (see et'Altere; Great Altere)

Firedrake: A dragon-like creature, about the size of a large falcon, used in hunting or sport. It can be trained to respond to whistles or other commands. It is fiercely loyal to its master and will die in protecting him or her. They cannot be bred in captivity and must be captured in the wild.

Flying Catlin: A winged feline-type animal bred in North Point and trained to deliver messages. Most are black and white striped, from ears to tail, with blue-black feathered wings. Sworn to its duty as messenger, it can also be playful, aloof, annoying, proud, and loveable. A confusing breed to be sure, they are not kept as pets due to their flighty nature.

Foreign Trade Minister: A member of the High Council, this person's main duty is to ensure trade between other countries and en'Edlia is fairly priced, safe for the consumer, and delivered undamaged. The minister travels to other countries to set up trade agreements for both imported and exported products. The minister must be versed in foreign customs, languages, and policies. In times of war, this position can be hazardous. Birth-gifts which can aid in these duties are speaking languages, x-ray vision and photographic memory. Currently in this position is Matriarch Birkin.

Fossi-shell: Shells of the fossi-snail which produce a blue phosphorescent glow which grows brighter the colder it gets.

Though mainly used for lighting am'Oran underwater cavern communities, they are also used as trade items, although not as effective out of the cold sea depths (see also Fossi-snail; am'Oran; am'Orans).

Fossi-snail: A type of deep-sea snail which imbues its shell with phosphorescence as it produces it. They are seeded and farmed by the am'Orans and used as a protein-rich food (see Fossi-shell).

Go-betweens: The interior corridors inside the walls between rooms which can only be entered through secret doorways known to the ruling family and its protectors. Often there are also small secret panels which can be moved to allow spying or safely peeking into a room while remaining unseen. These were created to give extra protection to the ruling family from interior threats, invasion, and also to provide faster means of travel between palace rooms when needed for safety or convenience.

Great Altere: The ruler of et'Alterens villages. Elected by the people, The Great Altere serves as ruler until death. Seen as both a spiritual and secular leader, he or she is treated with great respect and loyalty and has power to make laws, perform marriages, bless crops, and declare war among many other things (see et'Altere; et'Alterens).

High Commander: A member of the en'Edlian High Council, this person's main duty is to recruit, train, maintain, and deploy armed forces in the sworn duty to provide protection and help to the people of en'Edlia and its surrounding area. This includes smaller cities which are not under protection from any other country. The palace and local guards are included in this commander's force as he works with the High Keeper of the Peace. He has the added responsibility to recruit, train, maintain and deploy companies of soldiers in times of war. The high commander will then act as High Commander of the Land Forces under the High Council's direction. There are several birth-gifts which can aid in this duty, including impervious skin, teleportation of large masses and strengthening others. This position is currently held by Patriarch Kitzer.

High Council: The governing body of en'Edlia made up of twelve men and women including the high patriarch and high matriarch currently ruling. (see High Council Members)

High Council Members: This ruling body of twelve men and women of en'Edlia currently includes: High Patriarch Merrick; High Matriarch Narrian; Oracle—Patriarch Ardloh; High Mariner—Patriarch Cebton; High Commander-Patriarch Kitzer; Sea Merchant Council Rep.—Patriarch Royer; Land Merchant Council Rep.—Matriarch Shappel; City Council Rep.—Patriarch Pepperton; Foreign Trade Minister—Matriarch Birkin; High Keeper of the Peace—Patriarch Degler; Portal Guard Commander—Patriarch Olec; Scribe—Patriarch Cilcom (see each office individually for a description of position duties).

High Keeper of the Peace: A member of the en'Edlian High Council, this person's main duty is to maintain a peaceful environment in and around the city of en'Edlia, but extends to the whole country as well. The position is currently held by Patriarch Degler, who works with the portal guards, palace guards, and the high commander and his command.

High Mariner: A member of the en'Edlian High Council, this person's main duty is to ensure all ships are seaworthy, all crews are well treated. He is to report incidents of piracy, abuse of crew members, slavery, or incompetency in an admiralty, captainship, or any officers. He works with the Sea Merchants' Council to insure safe and adequate seafaring provisions for both the ships and the crews. He has an inspection crew which assists in the work. The high mariner has the added responsibility to recruit, train, maintain, and deploy a fleet of ships with their crews in times of war. The high mariner will then act as High Commander of the Sea Fleet under the High Council's direction. Several birth-gifts can aid in this duty, such as control of water, teleportation of large masses and breathing underwater. This position is currently held by Patriarch Cebton.

High Matriarch: The female leader of the realm of en'Edlia on the planet Irth. She is a member of the High Council and usually wife of the high patriarch. On some occasions the high patriarch will die and a new high patriarch will be chosen, usually eldest son from the ruling family. In these situations, the high matriarch retains her title until her death, and the wife of the new high patriarch is given the temporary title of crown matriarch.

High Patriarch: The male leader of the realm of en'Edlia on the planet Irth. He is the head of the high council. His wife is usually the high matriarch except in certain situations. The title position is usually handed down from father to eldest son, except when there is no son born to the ruling family. In which case, the eldest daughter becomes crown matriarch. In rare cases due to corruption, the people have cast out a high patriarch by majority vote, and chosen another to replace him (see Crown Matriarch; High Matriarch).

Hordle: A long-legged gentle animal the size of a large horse, with short, smooth hair, a long narrow head, floppy ears, and a long, slender tail which ends in a puff of hair. Its large, round eyes change color with the weather. Its feet are thickly padded on the bottom and end in six toes. The hair can be a variety of colors, including white, tan, pale yellow, chocolate-brown and black, but never more than one color on any single animal. Hordles were imported from Leppash to en'Edlia for the patriarchal family, specifically to pull the palace coaches. There are twelve all-white hordles in the palace stables currently.

Ichy-fruit: A soft, deliciously sweet fruit which can be eaten dried, raw, cooked, or made into sauce or juice. The fruit's hairy, pink and yellow striped skin produces an allergen which creates intense itching when rubbed on people's skin. One must be careful to wear protection when handling the fresh fruit and seek medical attention if contact occurs.

Irth's moons: am'Oranth and ul'Damen (see each individual listing for details)

Irth Star: A nocturnal bird which glows a soft yellow-orange. It has a long forked tail and slender wings. Often in large flocks, they are a spectacular sight, like swirling lights or dancing stars in the night sky.

King of the Sea Trolls: A legendary creature famous in many Irth children's tales. He ruled the sea trolls who controlled the seas and captured unsuspecting Irthians lost at sea. He was known for marrying an en'Edlian maiden who, though she loved him, could never find complete happiness under the sea. The king took his bride to live with him in his undersea kingdom. His heart was broken when she drowned trying to return to her family after living with him for many years.

Land Merchants' Council Representative: A member of the en'Edlian High Council, this person's main duty is to represent all the merchants, shopkeepers, business owners, and other entrepreneurs who do their business on land. Although some may import wares from overseas, they do not have ships or businesses involving exportation of merchandise overseas without having a representative on the Sea Merchants Council as well. The representative takes the voice of these merchants to the High Council. The Land Merchants' Council works with the Foreign Trade Minister and the Sea Merchants' Council to insure fair trade. This position is currently held by Patriarch Shappel.

Leppash: An inland city in the country of en'Edlia, with wide-spread rural farms and ranches on grassy plains and rolling hills. It is known for its magnificent animal breeding of creatures like hordles, bumpheads, and mozers which are highly prized and sought after on Irth (see Bumphead; Hordle; Mozer).

Mozer: A slow, gentle pasture dwelling animal raised primarily in Leppash. It is exported to other cities and countries for its meat, hide and production of sweetwater. Though not rare, it is highly valued and not usually afforded by the poorer classes of people (see Sweetwater).

Muffyberries: Bright yellow berries which are poisonous to humanoids until cooked. Used in breads and other dishes to add a sweet and sour flavor. The main food source for muffybirds and other fowl (see also Muffybirds; Muffybread).

Muffybird: A medium-sized bird which is a mass of tangled grey and brown feathers. With very short wings, beak and tail, it is hard to tell which end is which, especially when flying. It has a haphazard flight pattern and usually lands in a heap in a muffyberry bush. It is often seen in groups of three or four (see also Muffyberries).

Muffybread: A dense, whole grain bread made with muffyberries, nuts and seeds. A favorite breakfast food in en'Edlia (see also Muffyberries).

Matriarch: The title given to a female when she reaches adulthood, starts her own family through marriage, becomes a business woman, or owner of land or property. It is a common title like Mistress, Madam, or Lady, and not to be confused with the realm titles of high matriarch or crown matriarch (see High Matriarch; Crown Matriarch).

Off-worlder: Any being who is from another world outside the one you live on.

Oracle: Recognized as a spiritual leader and part of the High Council of en'Edlia. The oracle can be male or female and receives the office through the right of birth-gift. Very few are born with a birth-gift powerful enough to become oracle. Only one at a time may hold the office, usually the one with the strongest gift. Oracles can see into the future and have visions of things to come. They are sometimes ignored or considered a bit crazy by more contemporary thinkers. The current oracle is Patriarch Ardloh. The current oracle in training is Emija, a pre-matriarch.

os'Uron: A rough seaport city south of the city of en'Edlia, usually avoided by most other than scoundrels, scallywags, pirates, and cutthroats, or those looking for such characters.

Palm-bomb: A fist-sized black, tough-shelled fruit which is native to the tropical climates of Irth. The meat inside of the shell is pale pink, sweet and chewy, yet juicy, with a slight nutty flavor. The center is filled with a jelly which contains three large seeds. The seeds are poisonous and should not be eaten raw or cooked. The jelly is edible, though not recommended. If struck by a palm-bomb falling from a tree, it could render one unconscious or worse.

Pa'trees: A form of monetary exchange on Irth, pa'trees are coins made of brass-like metal. Their worth varies from country to country, but they are accepted as legal tender for purchases and payments.

Patriarch: The title given to a male once he reaches adulthood, becomes a head of household, owner of a business, land, or property. It is a common title like Sir, Mister, or Lord, and not to be confused with the realm title of high patriarch (see High Patriarch; Crown Patriarch).

po'Enay: A warm desert country across the sea from en'Edlia. There is open, friendly trade between the countries of po'Enay and en'Edlia and a few other countries and cities nearby. It is said that long, long ago a strange tall, black-skinned off-worlder came to en'Edlia, took a wife and left on a ship across the sea. It is believed the po'Enayans are their descendants and so related to those of en'Edlia as well (see map).

po'Enayans: The tall, slender, dark-skinned people of po'Enay. They have over-sized pointed ears, musical voices, and startling yellow eyes. Little clothing is needed in their home country, but when visiting the cooler climates, they wear long, flowing robes in bright, patterned colors of red, orange, yellow and blue. It is said they bring the desert sun and warmth with them. They have long, broad feet which help them navigate the desert sands. They never wear shoes. Their hair is the same color as their skin, a warm, deep-brown, and is worn very short for both males and females. Only the king and queen have long, plaited hair ornately wrapped around their heads and fastened with beautifully hand-carved ornaments of gold, shell, and bone.

Portal Guard Commander: A member of the en'Edlian High Council, this person's main duty is to maintain a watchful guard at all off-world portals and to open and close the portals which allow beings on and off Irth. This position is given to one whose birth-gift is the ability to open portals, but one must be proven loyal and trustworthy to obtain the office. With a company of men at his disposal, the commander must keep a constant vigil to protect the lives and safety of all of Irth. The commander also communicates and collaborates with the other Portal Guards in all other parts of Irth. The current person in this position is Patriarch Olec.

Rainbow Eel: A slender, sinuous fish with flashing rainbow colors along its sides. These colors are sloughed into the water and left in a trail when it is frightened, thus confusing its would-be attacker. It is considered good fortune to swim through an eel's rainbow trail. These eels are considered a delicacy in en'Edlia. Unfortunately the eel's lovely colors vanish when it dies, so eel skins are worthless.

Ruglump: A domesticated, gentle animal with long, soft hair, floppy ears and large brown eyes. They are plump and cozy, sleeping most of the time. They can occasionally be roused to action by the smell of food, and love to be petted and scratched all over. A favorite pet for young children, they come in varying sizes and colors, including purple and apricot.

Scribe: A member of the en'Edlian High Council, this person's duty is to take accurate notes during all council meetings, note the names of those present, and report or read back all notes from previous meetings as needed. The scribe is also responsible for the care, keeping, and copying of all notes, certificates of registered birth-gifts, patriarchal family genealogy, declarations, proclamations, laws, and other official documents of the realm of en'Edlia. The scribe may have others who assist him who have the appropriate birth-gifts and are approved by the High Council.

Sea Merchants' Council Representative: A member of the en'Edlian High Council, this person's duty is to represent all merchants whose businesses involve transporting products over the sea. They are to bring concerns, piracy issues, or other breaches of law to the attention of the High Council, whether it is by one of their own local council or one from a trade-treatied foreign country. The Sea Merchants' Council works with the Foreign Trade Minister and the Land Merchants' Council to insure fair trade.

Shell Fish: Tiny, silver and pink fish which find safety and shelter from predators in abandoned shells.

Sinepa: An inland city northeast of the city of en'Edlia known for its exotic flower and plant production. It exports bulbs, starts, cuttings, and whole plants to other cities and countries on Irth. It also imports foreign flora for the patriarchal gardens of the palace along with garden displays in other cities and countries. The Sinepa Scarlett Sconce was developed and named for this city (see Sinepa Scarlett Sconce).

Sinepa Scarlet Sconce: An intensely red, blooming plant developed in Sinepa. The leaves, stems, and roots of this plant are scarlet red. The lantern-like flowers are pure white with red veins and have an iridescent glow at night or in a dark room. They are often used along garden pathways or as part of a bouquet on a table during the evening meal.

Singing Sea Turtles: Gentle sea turtles which rarely grow larger than a soup bowl and emit the most melodious sounds which prove quite soothing to humanoids. They are often kept as pets, especially in sick-care houses. *Caution—these turtles can be dangerous!* When surrounded by a pod of these turtles, people have been known to drown because they relaxed so much they fell asleep in the water. Never keep more than one or two in the same place if you want to do anything but sleep. They are herded and raised as trade items by the am'Oran people (see am'Orans).

Skitters: Long-tailed, soft, furry animals which live in burrows in the foothills of the Altere Mountains. Their slender bodies, small rounded ears, large black eyes, and whiskered blue noses make these creatures popular pets. They are energetic, yet easily tamed. They make soft, whirring noises when petted. Children carry them wrapped around their necks or over their shoulders. Skitters are favorite bedtime partners and outdoor companions for both children and the elderly. The et'Alterens capture and tame them for trade.

Slappers: See Slapphierocious

Slapphierocious: Commonly called slappers, they are a biting, flying insect which are irritating but not extremely harmful unless swarmed by them. In that event, it is advisable seek medical attention. Their bite leaves a red swollen bump on the skin which itches mildly, unless you are allergic.

Slime snail: A giant sea snail which produces vast quantities of a slimy substance when removed from the sea. Ship builders gather these snails to waterproof the hulls of the ships before they are put into the sea for the first time. The snails are not harmed in this process and are returned to the sea when the job is finished. The only hazard of the process is the snails produce soft squeaking sounds when removed from the sea. It was long thought they were suffering, but research has shown the sound is made due to the huge amounts of slime being excreted from their bodies. The sound of over a hundred slime snails at work can be overwhelming; hence the ship builders are required to plug their ears with cloth during this process.

Spectar-cats: Compared to leopards of Earth, the spectar-cat is at least twice the size. These large felines have sleek, speckled coats of black, cream, and orange. Green eyes are most common. Though generally gentle in natural, they can be deadly if provoked. They are native to the Raden Islands and some areas of po'Enay. Spectars are bred on the islands to serve and to protect the royal family. Two spectar-cats can easily pull a cart with four adults in it about 25-30 miles in an hour without rest. There are also annual spectar-cat cart races which are highly competitive. These races are always won by the king of Raden, whether he deserves it or not.

Squirting Sea Plums: An underwater fruit which grows wild in most seas on Irth. It is a lovely deep reddish-purple color with a salty skin and sweet, fruity flesh. The plants will squirt a deep purple liquid when disturbed. After harvesting, the fruit will squirt its seeds out when firmly pinched. It is delicious raw, dried or cooked. Sea plum juice is an excellent thirst quencher. It has become one of the intentionally planted and harvested sea crops produced by the am'Orans and traded with others on Irth (see am'Orans).

Sweetwater: A watery, pale blue liquid produced by some female pasture animals, like bumpheads and mozers. Used to nurse their young, it is also gathered and made into tasty curds which are exported to other cities on Irth. Sweetwater can be a refreshing drink on its own, flavored with other fruit or vegetable juices, or poured over other foods (see Bumphead; Mozer).

The Shards: A small part of the city of en'Edlia where the extremely poor, broken, desperate, hopeless and wicked people live. There have been many attempts to clean and heal this section of the city, but it continues to fester with darkness and evil.

ul'Damen: The late rising second moon of Irth. Between it and am'Oranth, it is the brighter of the two. When full, it shines a gloriously brilliant orange-pink color. When setting, it deepens to a rusty-red. Some call ul'Damen the moon of love because of its warm color and late rising (see also am'Oranth).

Waterblimp: The hollow skin-husk of the bloat fish which, when dried and filled with water, becomes an excellent, easily breakable bomb for dousing unsuspecting victims. *Caution: Use at your own risk!* (see Bloat fish).

Xens: People of Irth who fear or are suspicious of off-worlders, especially in the ruling class. They have created a secret group which promotes civil uprising and recruits those especially dealing with dark magics. Their headquarters is in The Shards in the city of en'Edlia (see also Off-worlders; Dark Magic; The Shards).

Zippers: See Zipperzuli-benefactus

Zipperzuli-benefactus: Commonly known as zippers, they are small, neon-blue flying insects which help pollenate plant life on Irth. They are extremely fast moving and their tremendous wing-speed produces a buzzing sound. They produce zulijuice and are usually harmless to other creatures (see Zulijuice).

Zulijuice: A thick, sweet liquid produced by the zipperzuli-benefactus. It is clear pale-purple in color. Used in cooking and for sweetening drinks and other foods, and as food for other animals and insects, it serves as a salve for healing burns. There are zulijuice farms on Irth, particularly in Leppash (see map).

CHAPTER 1

The message came by catlin from Irth to Earth. The small black and white striped feline with bluish-black feathered wings was swift and sworn to its duty. However it was not above having a bit of fun in the process of its business.

Banking around Lyndell's castle towers, the catlin dove between the posted guards on the upper wall, yowling fiercely. The startled guards cried out in alarm and ducked for cover. The catlin then whisked up to the window of Merrick and Krystin's chambers. There it perched on the ledge for a moment, licking its paw and enjoying its view. Below, the spooked and cursing guards were shaking their fists, promising revenge.

The catlin stretched lazily, satisfied it had caused a sufficient stir, then leapt through the open window. It landed lightly on the floor behind the tapestry, which hung over the opening to keep out the cool spring air. Sauntering to the middle of the room, it yowled its greeting and announcement of the arrival of a message. It sat on its haunches, folded back its glossy wings, and waited to be noticed. The catlin switched its tail impatiently. If it had to yowl again, it might have to demand higher pay.

Presently, Princess Krystin came into the sitting room, yawning and rubbing her still sleepy green eyes. "I thought I heard a catlin," she said drowsily. She knelt down, her long golden-brown braid slipping over her shoulder. She opened the message tube which was attached to the animal's back by a leather harness. Pulling out a roll of parchment, she stroked the catlin gently.

"Merrick!" Krystin called toward the bedchambers. "A message from home."

Smiling, her husband, Merrick ambled into the sitting room. "Who's it from?" he asked, coming up from behind and putting his arms around her.

"I'm not sure," she replied, returning his smile and affection. "I've never seen this seal before."

Krystin turned and handed Merrick the rolled message. He glanced at the green wax seal which held it closed.

"It's the seal of en'Edlia's High Council," Merrick said running his hand through his dark hair. "It must be official business, though I can't imagine what it might concern." He tapped one side of the imprinted waxy glob and it vanished with a "poof." Merrick began to unroll the crisp parchment.

"Official business is boring," Krystin yawned. "I'll go see to the twins."

Merrick slumped into a soft chair. His brow furrowed as his dark eyes moved quickly over the words written in a flowing script. Suddenly he gasped, sitting bolt upright in the chair. "Oh, no," he moaned, dropping his face into his hand.

Krystin came back towing a toddler with each hand. Her husband sat limply, his face pale. "Merrick! What's the matter?" she cried. She released the children and knelt at Merrick's side, touching him gently.

"I'm being called back home to en'Edlia," Merrick choked out. He looked sadly into his wife's eyes. "My father is dead."

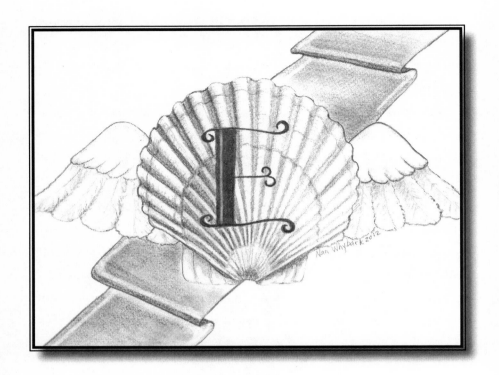

CHAPTER 2

"**K**rystin is coming! My new sister is coming!" Nizza couldn't stop saying it. "After twelve long years with just brothers, I'll have a sister living right here with me!"

Nizza turned a dancing circle, her arms wide and her long, straight, red hair flying out in all directions. "Can she sleep in my room, Mother?"

"No, dear," Narrian, the high matriarch of en'Edlia replied, a small smile touching her lips. "She'll be in the high patriarchal chambers with your brother, Merrick."

"Oh." Nizza frowned disappointedly. "I wish I could have gone to their wedding with you and father. Merrick always gets to do fun things."

"I'm sure Merrick will be having much less fun now he . . . he . . . ," Narrian tried to control her emotions. She drew a ragged breath as the tears came to her eyes yet again. Her unadorned white dress, a symbol of her mourning, lay around her like snow. Her dark hair was pinned up away from her face. "How can I ever go on without my dear, strong Brokt?" she muttered. "I'm overwhelmed with funeral preparations, the coronation ceremony, and all the foreign ambassadors and dignitaries coming from all over Irth and off-worlds to pay their respects. He was too young to leave me so soon."

"Oh, Mother," Nizza ran to sit beside her mother and place a loving arm around her shoulders.

Concentrating on radiating happiness toward her mother, Nizza envisioned a warming, golden glow around them both, easing their sorrow and carrying away the heaviness of heart they felt.

This was Nizza's birth-gift, a magical power which all people of Irth are born with. Each person's gift could be different. Each must learn to control and use it to help themselves and others. Nizza thought hers was perfect. She loved giving others happiness and peace, even though she wasn't affected by her own power. Her family's grief had been easier for her to bear knowing she could ease some of the harder moments for them, like now.

Nizza particularly liked using her birth-gift for defensive purposes. It was so satisfying watching her brothers squirm. They loved to tease and pester her, using their own birth-gifts of levitation and controlling insects to play jokes on her or try to anger her. However, Nizza's gift had proven an equal match, for Jarrius and Wayen soon found themselves crying with happiness, helpless under her power.

Now as she sat by her lonely, grieving parent, she felt her mother relax as the deep sorrow was lifted by her gift. As she continued to comfort the high matriarch, Nizza thought about what was happening in en'Edlia.

Third born and only daughter of High Patriarch Brokt and High Matriarch Narrian, Nizza had watched the palace, and the realm alike, tumble into political upheaval. Her oldest brother, Crown Patriarch Merrick, was to claim the throne at the death of their father. He was coming home after five years on the portal world of Earth with an off-world wife and two-year-old twin daughters. There had never been an off-worlder in the high patriarchal family line in the history of en'Edlia. Never.

The High Council feared rebellion from the Xens. Xens were purists believing only those of Irth should be allowed into the high patriarchal family. Guardwatch on the ruling family had been increased. The city council was doing all it could to calm the citizens of en'Edlia in the midst of this turmoil.

So many events were happening and each inspiring different emotions for Nizza. She felt joy at Merrick's return, and the prospect of having a sister close. She felt deep sorrow at her beloved father's death. There was hope for relief of en'Edlia's building tension and the return to peace as the new high patriarch was accepted and gained control.

Nizza would have to be careful to choose wisely when and where to use her birth-gift. Overuse of one's gift could cause total exhaustion, unconsciousness, mind-sickness or even death. Nizza didn't actually know anyone who had died, but the history books had recorded proper warnings of those who had.

For now, all those feelings were slinking off into the murky background of her mind as the happiness she generated began to soak in and her mother began to smile again.

"Mother, when will I get to meet my new sister?" Nizza asked anxiously, her excitement about Merrick's return surfacing again.

"His catlin message said they would be here tomorrow morning, dear," Narrian replied. "And thank you." She gave Nizza a squeeze. "Just don't wear yourself out. We will get through this together."

"I know we will," Nizza replied quietly. "I just want to help. I hate feeling useless."

"Well, then," her mother said rising. "Let's go see what we can be doing instead of just sitting here." She led Nizza out of the bedchamber and down the hall toward the kitchens.

CHAPTER 3

S mich sat on the wall dangling his legs as he held two waterblimps carefully concealed under his coat. He was supposed to meet his cousin, Wayen, here so they could watch the arrival of Crown Prince Merrick, but Smich was early. He couldn't wait to get away from his grieving family. It was all so gloomy. He would be glad when the funeral was over. He hated things like that. He sighed as he thought of his mother, her eyes red from crying. He had to get away. He couldn't stand to see her that way.

Looking off into the distance, Smich remembered a time he had had with his Uncle Brokt. It had been his uncle who had shown him just how to dry the bloat fish skin to a delicate crispness, and then fill it with water. It was his uncle who had taken him up on one of the palace tower walks and, with several waterblimps in hand, they had bombarded a group of unsuspecting guards.

Smich chuckled. He couldn't wait to see Wayen's face when he showed him the bulging waterblimps! What a perfect tribute to good old Uncle Brokt! He and Wayen would have to seriously discuss who should be the receivers of such wonderful presents. Smich smiled mischievously. It was going to be an exciting day.

*   *   *

Nizza lay sleeping deeply in her bed which was suspended by thick ropes from the lofty ceiling. It was like a giant swing which rocked her gently to sleep each night. However, she had lain awake into the single hours of the watch, not able to sleep for her excitement at the return of her brother and his family. After she did finally drift off, she had a strange dream . . .

The towers of en'Edlia's palace were before her as she looked up. Suddenly a new tower rose up, beautiful, yet strange and different from all the other towers. Nizza admired the new tower's graceful lines, its unique design. It seemed to have an inner strength. It was truly wonderful.

Just as suddenly as the tower had risen up, great black clouds gathered overhead and thunder rumbled menacingly. Nizza felt fear without knowing why. She had never feared storms before. The clouds continued to gather as the thunder's booming began to grow more intense. A flash of lightning lit the sky. Nizza was momentarily blinded as she cowered before the angry storm. She felt the new tower was in great danger. It made no sense, but she ran toward the palace screaming words of warning to the beautiful tower.

Lightning arched down from the sky, striking the tower with terrifying force. Nizza opened her mouth to scream but the roaring thunder and crackling lightning drowned out her voice. Again and again the bolts struck the tower, chipping away at its beauty as it created black scars and broken stones. Nizza watched the falling debris as the storm seemed bent on the tower's destruction. She wanted to protect it, to shelter it somehow, but the tower was surrounded by all the other towers. It was unreachable and the storm was so huge. She felt very small and helpless. She looked for someone to help her. She finally noticed her brother, Merrick inside the iron gate which opened in the high walls which surrounded the palace towers. She called out to him, pointing at the storm, but he shut the gate tightly. Then he turned his back to her and vanished. She frantically called and looked for others to help. There was no one.

Then suddenly Nizza was surrounded by crowds of people and her heart leaped with hope the tower could now be saved. She turned to see who had come to help, and as she looked, the faces in the crowd grew angry and dark as the storm. They rushed forward and began hurling rocks at the tower, yelling mean, hurtful things. Nizza tried to stop them. She tried to tell them about the tower's beauty. No one listened. No one stopped. Nizza was pushed and shoved aside as tears streamed down her face. "No!" she cried as she fell to the ground. "No! No! Nooooo . . . ."

*　　*　　*

Wayen fidgeted as his man-servant, Heatham, fussed over his formal clothes, tucking in his shirt yet again. Heatham adjusted his jacket and gold sash which designated him as an heir in the ruling family. Wayen hated all the formal occasions and this was no exception. He didn't mind his brother, Merrick, coming home; he just minded having to dress up for it. He was the youngest and was somewhat spoiled, but that suited him fine.

"Enough, Heatham!" Wayen stepped back out of reach. "I am old enough to fix my own clothes now. I'll be ten at the next season, you know."

"As you wish, young master," Heatham bowed, frowning. "But if the high matriarch docks my wages because you are unkempt, I shall require compensation from your pocket, sir." Heatham straightened his own clothes, turned smartly on his heel, and strode briskly out of the room.

Wayen was glad to be rid of him. He was stuffy and old and smelled like a rainbow eel. *Come to think of it, Heatham kind of looks like one too.* Wayen grinned. It would be worth losing a few coins to see less of Heatham.

Wayen frowned as he suddenly found his father's words drifting through his thoughts. *"Son, you must treat others with kindness no matter their station or position. It will mark you as a truly great leader. Even though you are my youngest, you will have many opportunities to lead and even rule. Never abuse those who serve you."*

Sighing, Wayen flopped down on a chair. *Why did you have to leave me now, Father,* he thought. *I need you.* He felt lost and miserable as he let his thoughts wander.

Moments later, he stomped his foot. He might be the baby of the family, but he didn't want to be seen acting like one. He used his anger to push away his tender feelings. He needed to be on with his own plans for the morning.

He had to make an appearance with the family, of course. Then he could sneak away to find his cousin, Smich for the welcoming procession. From a box deep in his clothes cupboard, he pulled out the last things he needed and stuffed them into his pockets. This might turn out to be a good day after all.

*   *   *

The morning sun was veiled through the bedchamber window's sheer fabric. The sky was clear. A gentle breeze blew in from the sea. The sea birds shrieked in the distance as they fought over breakfast. Nizza gasped and sat up, pushing her way dreamily out of sleep. She was moist with sweat and could feel her heart pounding in her chest. She lay back, closing her eyes again. Her strange dream, so real a moment ago, was quickly fading from her memory. She helped it go by trying to think of more pleasant things.

Abruptly, her eyes flew open again. This was the day! Merrick would be here today!

Nizza threw back the covers, suddenly too warm, and rolled out of bed nearly crashing to the floor in her haste. *What time could it be?* As if knowing her need, one of the hour-men walked past her chambers calling out, "Eight and a quarter bells! Eight and a quarter bells!"

"Oh, no!" Nizza gasped. "I'm late!" She threw open one of her large wooden trunks and began digging through her clothes. "What should I wear?" she cried.

She ran to her clothes cupboard, then scurried back to her bedside and pulled twice on the long, gold cord which rang a bell calling her maids.

In minutes she was surrounded by three women bustling about. Murm had brought breakfast on a tray. It was steamed squirting sea plums with sweetwater and fresh muffybread. Boolie swept into the room with Nizza's emerald-green satin and lace dress and clean underclothes. Nizza loved the dress even though Wayen told her it looked like it was made of seaweed.

And finally Leesel, Nizza's favorite maid, set down the pitcher of washing water and began brushing out her hair. "Oh, please can you braid it, Leesel?" Nizza begged. "But no ribbons! I want to look more grown-up today."

"As you wish, young mistress," Leesel replied warmly. She began tugging on Nizza's hair with strong, skilled fingers, braiding her long, red tresses.

Leesel called Nizza "young mistress" whenever she wished to sound formal, but it was meant to tease her. Nizza considered Leesel her auntie, though there was no blood relation between them. She knew she could always depend on her faithful maid for anything, like keeping secrets, sneaking in a piece of cake at bedtime or covering for her if she was absent without her parents' knowledge. Those days were coming to an end as Nizza was twelve now. In only two years she would be at an age to begin a courtship. Nizza sighed at the thought, then shrieked as Boolie doused her with warm water for her washing.

After gulping down breakfast and wrestling into her clothes, Nizza was off down the hall with her maid still running behind her finishing the last of her long braid. Finally, just as Nizza reached the stairs, Leesel grabbed her braid bringing her to a howling halt.

"What did you do that for?" cried Nizza, rubbing her head.

"Because you have to stand still for this part," Leesel replied.

"Oh . . . very well."

With a couple of flips and a twirl, Leesel whipped the braid up in an elegant twist and pinned it in place with a beautifully delicate seashell comb.

"Merrick will be happy to see you wear his gift," her maid stated, still fussing over her hair and clothes.

"Can I go now? I really am late."

Leesel smiled and curtsied. "As you wish, young mistress," she replied dipping her head respectfully.

"Oh, Leesel, do stop!" Nizza gave her a quick hug, turned, and flew down the long staircase just as the tower bells began to chime the hour, echoing through all of en'Edlia.

CHAPTER 4

Portal Commander Olec opened the portal between Earth and Irth with his birth-gift. It was a rare, treasured gift in en'Edlia. Olec was proud to serve his country in this way. He stood tall and straight in his white dress uniform with an emerald-green sash, gold braid trim, and buttons. As he held open the portal entrance for the crown patriarch and his family, long golden trumpets sounded their arrival. Olec saluted with his hand over his heart as he bowed before them.

In the town center, the trumpets' four-note blast echoed off the palace walls. The first cheer from the people went up in answer, echoing back. Pushing aside their grief at the loss of their beloved High Patriarch Brokt, en'Edlians took the opportunity for joy at Merrick's return.

After crossing through the portal, Krystin delightedly inspected and petted the unusual animals called hordles harnessed to the splendid deep-green palace coach.

"The hordles," Krystin was told by the coach driver, "are imported from Leppash especially for the ruling family." She was enraptured by these long-legged gentle animals, but couldn't decide if they looked more like dogs or horses. They had short hair, long narrow heads, floppy ears, and a long tail which ended in a puff of hair. Their large, round eyes changed color with the weather. On this sunny day, their eyes were brilliant green.

"Amazing!" Krystin cried. The twins laughed as they felt the hordles' soft white coats. Then they were quickly ushered into their seats.

The coachman whistled and the coach lurched forward as the six white hordles began to move. They set off at a brisk pace. The hordles feet were many-toed with thickly calloused pads. They made almost no sound on the dirt lane which soon turned to cobblestone paving.

Krystin was astounded by all the new sights. She turned and twisted trying to see everything, all while holding one of the squirming twins also struggling to see.

Merrick chuckled. "The people will think you are just a curious child." First impressions were the strongest and Merrick knew the importance of this event.

'Well, all right," Krystin replied. "I'll try to act like a princess, even though I feel like this curious child." She smiled, hugging her daughter gently.

"Soon to be crown matriarch!" Merrick reminded her. He squeezed her hand at her worried look. "You'll be just perfect. I promise to show you all around en'Edlia once we get settled."

Krystin's smile returned. "I hope the children will be happy here." *I hope I'll be happy here*, she thought to herself.

Merrick was worried too. He had been comfortable enough in Lyndell on Earth. The people had accepted him relatively well after he had rid them of an evil sorceress and her enchanted dragon. He had become a regular sight around the castle and in the castle-city of Dayn.

In the five years he had been gone from en'Edlia as Earth's foreign ambassador, there had been few trips home. Those had been only to make his report to the high counsel and his father. Coming back now under such circumstances was not what he had hoped for. He felt a stab of sorrow pierce his heart as he thought of his grieving mother, alone now, and the empty space in his life which would no longer be filled by his father. He was worried about how the people would accept his new family. *What could Krystin possibly do to endear the people to her? What could she bring to my world which would help it?*

He glanced over at his wife. She was so happy, beautiful, and naïve. He smiled as he felt his love for her tighten his chest. She would have to be protected. He hoped his mother would be able to help. It was going to be uncomfortable and hard for a while. He would be busy with the affairs of the realm a great deal of the time. His family was grieving and Krystin would be lonely and homesick.

Merrick felt a small hand on his and a tug on his sleeve. He pushed his worry into the back of his mind as he looked down into the face of his two-year old daughter, Jewl, all aglow with excitement. "Wha dat, Dada?" she squealed. "Wha dat?"

Lifting Jewl to his lap, he held her close, joining his family's excitement at being on Irth for the first time.

Krystin had never seen such amazing sights. Dragons flew through the air, not just one, but many in all different colors. Some had riders, others were accompanied by their young. The sun gleamed off their scales like gems.

Sea birds wheeled in the sky, calling out their greetings. Other birds with such spectacular multi-colored plumage flitted overhead. Krystin could hardly believe they were real. Jewl squealed and clapped her hands, pointing to a flying purple pony. "Horsey, Momma!" she called out excitedly.

Not only creatures filled the skies, but people as well. Some floated in a single spot, while others glided along following the course of the coach. Krystin felt like she was in a fantastic dream.

Beautiful flowers and trees lined the road they traveled. Huge yellow blooms with trumpet-like pestles bobbed as they sent their sweet fragrances on the breeze. Smaller, scarlet-red plants with white lantern-like flowers glowed under the shade trees. Deep-purple bell flowers hung from creeping plants which coiled around some of the trees. Krystin thought she heard them chiming as the carriage went past.

The trees were filled with singing birds, while many branches hung heavy with fruit. There were plump, white, nearly pear-shaped fruits, and some long, narrow pale-green pods. Still other fruits, like deep-pink pancakes, moved with the slightest breeze, seemingly light as a feather.

"Wait till you see the palace gardens!" remarked Merrick. "I hope Tesh is still gardener there. He is amazing!"

As they drew ever nearer the palace, the sharp, salty smell of the sea became more distinct. Krystin breathed it in, smiling, refreshed by the crisp cool air. She had never seen the sea, but Merrick's tales made her long for a glimpse of its sparkling waves and the feel of the warm sand on her bare feet. She wondered if it would even be allowed now that she was to be crown matriarch. That thought was brief as new sights came into view.

*　　*　　*

Nizza was out of breath by the time she skidded up next to her younger brother. His real name was Wayendolus, but everyone call him Wayen. Nizzarian was her given name though she much preferred Nizza. Her cousin, Nostronosmich, went by Smich, which fit him much better. She was sure he was lurking somewhere, planning mischief.

Someday Smich would be a patriarch in charge of his father's lands and estate. To her, Smich would always be Smich, no matter what.

After the formal greeting to all the foreign and visiting guests by the high patriarchal family, they gathered at the front of the palace to watch for and welcome Crown Patriarch Merrick and his family. The people of en'Edlia were very eager indeed to see this strange off-world woman with no magical birth-gift. Some were merely curious. What would she look like? Would she have green skin or many eyes? Would she have many hands to make up for her lack of magical ability? How could Merrick love such a creature?

Many were angered the crown patriarch would dare marry an off-worlder. If he was to rule in his father's stead, what kind of heir would he have? Could they even allow such a thing? They could never consider a leader with no birth-gift! It would be a crime against all Irth.

Some were uncertain. The unknown was always frightening. What if this new matriarch was so different no one could understand her? What if she brought with her new rules or changes to their way of life? Was this the beginning of a whole new cultural upheaval? What customs had she brought from her world to impose upon them? It seemed all of en'Edlia held its breath and waited.

*   *   *

Wayen shinnied up the wall and plopped down beside Smich. The two boys grinned at each other, very pleased with their vantage point and opportunity for mischief. Wayen knew Smich could relieve his gloom over his father's death. It had been nearly suffocating at the palace and he needed some release for his pent up emotions.

Smich revealed the waterblimps under his jacket as his cousin hooted for joy. He passed one to Wayen who quickly tucked it away. Their heads immediately went together as they discussed strategy and possible targets. This was going to be a great day!

CHAPTER 5

T he noise of the huge crowd grew so loud Jewl and Phyre were frightened and clung to their parents. As Merrick and Krystin smiled out the windows and waved their greetings, the couple could see that not all the faces were smiling back.

Merrick's concern grew as protest signs began to appear at the fringes of the throng. The crowd's roar continued to grow as the coach drew nearer. Signs on poles and in hands bounced up and down from various places, some just floated in the air. A united chanting began to come into focus in time with the bobbing signs. He gasped, and then was filled with anger at the unkind and threatening words.

"No M.O.W.s! No M.O.W.s! No M.O.W.s!" The chanting became louder. Fists were raised in the air by sign-holders and others around them. The words on the signs became clear.

"No M.O.W.s" some read. "DON'T *'MOW'* OUR RULERS" others declared. "PURITY OR NOTHING" still others demanded.

He tried to redirect Krystin's view away from them as much as possible, but still she caught sight of them.

"What is that?" she yelled in Merrick's ear, trying to make herself heard. "What does that mean?"

Merrick shook his head and shrugged as if he couldn't make out what she said. Inside he groaned, wondering how he could tell Krystin some of his people were not happy she was here.

Suddenly a person in a deep-blue hood appeared at the coach window. "NO M.O.W.s!" he yelled, instantly throwing a handful of sloppy mud into the coach splattering everything inside. "Purity or nothing!" Just as suddenly he was gone again.

Krystin gasped and cried out as the children began to cry, their little faces flecked with mud.

"GUARDS!" Merrick bellowed as he tried to brush the mud from Jewl's clothes.

A stern-looking female soldier peered in the coach. "My apologies, Crown Patriarch! Palace Guard Commander Arreshi, at your service!" she saluted then continued. "We had hoped the protective force field would not be needed so soon. I will implement it at once and call for a cleaner!"

There was a soft popping sound and a thin film appeared around the entire coach. It was pink at first then quickly paled to crystal clear. Krystin reached out to touch it. It gave her fingers a tingling sensation and hardly moved at her touch. She thought it strange it did not dampen the noise of the crowd at all.

The cleaner arrived moments after and with a twirl of his fingers, all their clothing and the coach's interior were like new again, including Jewl's not-so-fresh diaper. Phyre clapped her hands and cried, "More, Dada! More!" While Krystin shook her head in amazement, she hoped there was a cleaner or two at the palace.

"What is all that about?" Krystin questioned Merrick again. "What do they mean by M.O.W.s?"

Merrick frowned, clearing his throat nervously. "Just some environmental problems," he shouted over the noise, waving it off and smiling slightly. He turned back to his own window, hiding his concern from his wife. "I'll have to deal with this very soon," he said quietly to himself.

Krystin gave up trying to ask Merrick any more questions as the coach circled the city square and headed for the palace. Bright insignia flags showing a winged, white and gold seashell on a field of green were more numerous among the crowd than the protesters' signs. The large flags on poles lined the square, snapping smartly in the breeze. Above each one flew a smaller white flag in honor of the passing of Merrick's father, a sign the whole country was in mourning.

As the coach moved up the grand, wide drive in front of the palace, servants rushed to hold the reins of the hordles and open the doors of the coach. Krystin felt the force field move from the coach to form a shield at their backs as they moved away.

The regal couple, each holding a child, stepped out onto lush, green matting that ran from the drive down a long walkway, up a wide expanse of steps to an elegant veranda with pillars and lush floral displays, and beyond.

An enormous flag of the realm was displayed from a second story balcony; it too was over hung by a smaller white flag. The palace spires all supported green insignia flags and white flags as well. Krystin drew in a breath at the grandeur of it all. Lyndell had never been so glorious and beautiful. It made her feel humble, like a peasant girl in the presence of a king.

The walkway was lined with visitors, some extending their wishes of both welcome and condolences. Merrick lifted Phyre into his arms as they moved through this sea of people toward their waiting family on the veranda. Feeling very overwhelmed by the immense crowd and all the formalities, Krystin became shy, holding tightly onto Merrick's arm, while clinging to Jewl by her hand.

"You remember Portal Guard High Commander Olec," Merrick said, introducing Krystin as they went. Krystin had to release her grip on her husband to hold her hand over her heart and curtsy as Merrick had shown her before they came.

"Commander Olec," the matriarch nodded slightly. "An honor to meet you again," she commented politely. "Thank you for insuring our safe passage between portals. You have a miraculous gift."

The Commander snapped off a respectful salute and then bowed. "Thank you," he said quietly. "I only live to serve."

"Patriarch Degler, High Keeper of Peace," Merrick introduced the next in line. Stepping in close to Degler, he whispered, "I will want your report immediately after this ceremony. Do not delay." Degler paled slightly but nodded. The crown patriarch gave him a tight smile, then continued down the line of dignitaries. He then introduced each of the high council members in turn as they continued.

"This is, at last, our esteemed oracle, Ardloh," Merrick finished with a bow to the oracle.

Ardloh huffed and grabbed Merrick up in a hug nearly lifting him off his feet.

"So good to have you home at last! My deepest sympathies on your father's passing. We must talk soon!" puffed the oracle. "Let me introduce my apprentice, Emija."

Emija bowed and then smiled, sweeping her blonde hair off her shoulders. She was very short next to the towering oracle. Wearing the brown robe of an apprentice, she seemed plain next to the other dignitaries. But her deep, green eyes were bright with intelligence and hidden power.

"Emija is a rare gem!" Ardloh said proudly. "She has two birth-gifts! I must tell you more about her."

"Perhaps a bit later, Ardloh," Merrick cut in quickly. "We must be moving on."

"I would love to get to know you better, Emija," Krystin spoke up. "Will you come to the palace with the oracle sometime?"

"May we?" Emija turned to her teacher.

"What? Oh, yes, of course," Ardloh responded.

Nodding respectfully to Emija, Merrick smiled. "My condolences for having to put up with the honorable oracle."

Emija giggled, but Ardloh's face grew dark. "If you continue to call me 'the honorable oracle' I may have to put a jinx on you. You know I detest all those formalities!" He huffed again, and then grinned, his good nature returning. "Lovely little woman you have there," he winked at Merrick.

Merrick nodded, his face not reflecting Ardloh's seemingly carefree manner.

"Your daughters are beautiful," remarked Emija smiling warmly. The proud parents smiled and thanked her. Then turning, Merrick guided Krystin and the children on as his feelings of dread increased.

Krystin's head was whirling with names and faces as she neared Merrick's family on the veranda. No one she had met seemed different from those on her world, until she was introduced to the foreign ministers.

The pair from po'Enay were at least seven feet tall, dark-skinned, and slender. Their warm-brown braided hair piled on top of their heads was adorned with carved bone, shells, and small gold discs. Krystin had never seen a real shell before and had to ask Merrick what they were. She marveled at the po'Enayan's long colorful robes, pointed ears, startling yellow eyes, and musical voices. Their homeland was far across the sea to the south and had a warm, dry climate. They had formed an alliance with en'Edlia to enable trade between their countries. Krystin paused to listen to their pleasant accent, but finally had to move with Merrick along the nearly endless line.

Another group of foreigners included the five from the am'Oran undersea cavern cities. Krystin openly stared at these small delegates. They looked like children in size and build, but their large, deeply intelligent eyes and nasal, bubbling speech showed they were anything but children. Thick white hair, some long, some short, stood straight out from their heads. Krystin wasn't sure if the length of the hair was a sign of gender since they all dressed alike. They wore greenish-brown tight fitting leggings with short roughly-woven tops. Their skin was pale blue, nearly transparent in places and their noses were small, flat bumps with nostril slits. Krystin shuddered when she caught sight of the gill flaps down both sides of their necks.

"Merrick!" she whispered fiercely. "What are those things on their necks?"

"Don't worry," Merrick whispered back, patting her hand as she clung to him. "The am'Orans live in huge, caves under the sea. They have gills like fish for breathing under water as well as lungs for use on land."

"Oh," was all Krystin could say. *This land is very different from Lyndell, and stranger by the minute,* she thought to herself. *Will I ever be able to learn and understand all these new things?*

With great relief, Krystin reached the veranda and after curtseying low to the high matriarch of en'Edlia, happily flew into the arms of her mother-in-law. "Oh, Narrian," she cried. "I'm so sorry for the loss of dear Brokt. He was so sweet to me at the wedding. I shall always remember his kindness and love when the twins were born too."

Narrian hugged her tightly and whispered, "Thank you, Krystin. He did love you very much. He was always proud of Merrick's choice in making you his bride. How are you holding up?"

"I'm scared," Krystin whispered back. "I shall never measure up to you or be worthy of this great responsibility!"

Narrian gently pushed Krystin back, looking into her face. "From the moment I met you when we came to your Earth," Narrian began, "I could tell you were destined for greatness, my dear daughter. Hold your head high and smile. We all have fears from time to time. We will get through this together."

Krystin hugged her again as her eyes stung with tears. She regained her composure and smiled as she released the high matriarch.

Then it was Merrick's turn to embrace his mother. He held her tenderly for a long time, as tears sprung into both their eyes. "Oh, Mother," he whispered. "How we shall miss the old man!" His voice caught in his throat. He sent his thoughts of sorrow to her mind as he could not find the words to speak.

"It is good to have you home at last, my son," the high matriarch spoke with deep emotion. "How I have missed you!"

Mother and son stood in each other's arms a moment longer, struggling to compose themselves in front of the many guests. They wiped their eyes and Narrian straightened her golden-shell tiara she wore for formal occasions. Finally, they stepped apart, but stood with arms linked, still longing for more closeness and comfort in their grief.

"We will talk more later," Narrian quietly told Merrick, who nodded in response, placing his warming hand over his mother's.

She seems so frail and yet so strong, thought Merrick to himself. *I must be strong for her as well, as I know Father would have wanted.*

No sooner had Krystin turned to meet the rest of the family, than she was nearly knocked off her feet by a flying mass of braided red hair in a green satin dress.

"My new sister!" Nizza nearly screamed as she clung to Krystin. "Oh, I'm so happy to finally meet you!"

Krystin breathlessly tried to pry herself loose from the arms squeezing the air out of her. She pulled away, trying to see the face under all that beautiful, red hair.

Merrick had to smile as he witnessed his sister grab Krystin like a mountain she-bear. Nizza was nearly a grown woman. *When did that happen?* he wondered, amazed at the changes in her.

"I see you've met my little sister," Merrick remarked to his wife.

"I'm trying to," gasped Krystin.

Loosening her grip, Nizza looked up finally and gasped. "You are just as beautiful as mother said! I'm Nizza and now we are sisters! Do you have any other sisters? I don't! You're the only one," she said all in one breath.

Laughing and drawing Nizza back into her arms, Krystin replied, "I had a sister once, but she died when I was very little. I don't even remember her. I'm so glad to have a new sister. We will have to spend much time together getting to know each other."

"Oh, I do hope so!" Nizza gushed, grinning broadly. Then turning to her brother, she said solemnly, "It's about time you came home, Merrick." She gently laid her hand on his shoulder. She let some of her birth-gift flow into him, soothing the raw edges of the loss he was feeling. "We'll spend some time together too," she said as she hugged him.

CHAPTER 6

Smich burst through the doors into the royal sitting room where the family was sitting in quiet conversation. "That was intense! Did you see all the protestors? I thought a couple of them were going to start throwing things." Smich finally glanced around at the other faces in the room. Only then did he notice the lack of smiles.

"This is going to get wild! Isn't it?" he continued, trying to get a reaction to match his own enthusiasm.

Narrian stood quickly, facing him. "Nostronosmich!"

Smich cringed at the use of his full name. He knew now he had done something wrong, but was not sure what.

Seeing her nephew's face pale, Narrian softened her tone. "Smich, we need to help our new matriarch feel welcome and at home." Her eyes widened pointedly at him, indicating what he was doing was not in harmony with that.

"Oh," he said, his face now flushing red. "I . . . I'm sorry, Aunt Narrian, I guess I didn't think . . . ."

"As usual!" Wayen commented under his breath. Narrian gave him a piercing glance.

"Now," the high matriarch continued smoothly. "I think we could all use some refreshments on this warm day." She was used to handling difficult situations and taking charge. "Smich, would you be so kind as to pull the service cord."

Smich dropped his head and shuffled over to the corner of the room where a golden rope hung from an ornate hole in the wall. He gave it an unenthusiastic yank and slumped into a chair apart from the others.

"Wayen," Narrian turned toward her son, "Perhaps you and Smich would rather go straight to the kitchens for your food."

Wayen could hear in her tone it was not a suggestion, it was a command.

"Of course, Mother," he said with a small smile, his eyes throwing daggers at Smich. Wayen crossed the room hurriedly and took Smich roughly by the arm. "Come, cousin," he said through gritted teeth. "Let's go to the kitchens."

Wayen hauled the defeated Smich out of the room, just as the servants bustled in with trays of finger foods and drinks. Smich looked back longingly at the food as he allowed his cousin to escort him out.

When they had turned the corner at the end of the long hall, Wayen stopped suddenly and whirled toward Smich. "What were you thinking? Oh, that's right," he continued sarcastically, "you weren't! Merrick's wife doesn't know about any of this. He is trying not to frighten her the very first day she is here. Then you come in running your mouth off! Great slimy sea slugs! When will you learn to listen first and then speak?"

Smich leaned dejectedly against the wall and took his cousin's tongue lashing. He knew he deserved it. He just couldn't see why it was such a big deal. Better to just tell Merrick's wife straight up and be done with it. At least that's the way he saw it. He thought back to the chanting crowd, the angry looks, and the clenched fists punching the air. To him it was all blood-racing excitement. He grinned sheepishly as he recalled the waterblimp he had delivered anonymously to the head of one of the protestors.

"But it was fun when that protester got the waterblimp square on the noggin, wasn't it, Wayen?" He glanced at his cousin, hoping to break the tension.

Wayen face was scrunched in a frown. Suddenly his eyes closed and he shook his head. "You're hopeless, do you know that, Smich? Completely hopeless!" Wayen chuckled and put his arm around Smich steering him toward the kitchen again.

"And you're beginning to sound like your mother," Smich teased him.

They grinned broadly and were soon laughing together as they recalled the glories of the waterblimping and the reactions of their victims.

* * *

The next few weeks were very full ones for Merrick. His father's funeral had been long and tearful as thousands of en'Edlia's residents came to say goodbye to their beloved leader and friend, High Patriarch Broktomerris. The formalities lasted three days and the ruling family was exhausted.

The next week Crown Patriarch Merrickobrokt had been accepted as high patriarch by the majority vote of the people through the high council. The formal coronation had happened just two days after that. Immediately Merrick had to undertake the business of the realm. Long days and short nights, snatched bits of meals and conversations were his daily fare. He very much missed the rather carefree time he had spent in Lyndell. He wished his brother, Jarrius, was here to support him and at least listen to his complaints about how en'Edlia had changed in his absence.

However, Jarrius had quickly departed with regrets after the funeral and the coronation. He felt he had to return to his off-world ambassadorship on Quewyn and the complicated trade negotiations he was involved in. It would be months, more likely years, before he could return home for any lengthy period of time. Jarrius deemed it his duty, especially since their father had commissioned him to it.

Besides all that, Merrick worried about his family, as his time for his wife and daughters became moments. Fortunately for Krystin, Nizza had taken her and the twins under her wing. Nizza was intent in her self-proclaimed duty to show her new sister everything in the palace and round about it. Sometimes that worried Merrick even more.

CHAPTER 7

"Now," whispered Nizza to Krystin one late morning after the twins had been put down for their nap under the watchful care of Leesel. "We are going to explore the secret places which only our family knows."

"We had some places like that in Lyndell. I spent enough time there to last a lifetime." She looked nervously at Nizza. "Are we going to get wet?"

"Wet?" Nizza said surprised. "We are not going to the bay or down into the underwater caverns, we're just going to do a little spying," Nizza explained conspiratorially. "Come on, it'll be fun!"

"All right, lead on then, little Rateek!

"Who? What did you call me?"

"Oh, just a friend from the castle you reminded me of just then," Krystin said with a grin. "Let's go."

Nizza led her from the main hall near the patriarchal quarters, down the central staircase, along another long hallway, and into a large room filled with musical instruments. Krystin was fascinated with the bright metal horns, tiny stringed harps, and large decorated drums. She wanted to touch everything. "What are all these things?" she asked Nizza.

"Just some old instruments. Nothing important. We can come back and look at them again if you like. I could even get someone to play them for you."

"Could you?" Krystin's eyes widened. "That would be wonderful! I should like that very much. Thank you, Nizza."

"This way now. Come on!" Nizza called.

The girls threaded their way through all the chairs and music stands to one corner of the room where Nizza stopped in front of the patterned sky-blue draperies which covered the entire wall from the ceiling to the floor.

Krystin came up beside her with a questioning look on her face, but Nizza spoke up before she had time to ask. "No we didn't come here to see instruments or draperies. We came here to see what's behind them!" She drew back the drapes in the corner to reveal a hidden door.

Visions of damp, cramped tunnels suddenly filled Krystin's mind. She could mentally hear the echoes of the mocking laughter of Ditz, the gremlin, as she remembered the Lyndell castle lift door closing, leaving her and David trapped in total darkness. She shivered at the memory. "What's behind the door?" Krystin asked.

"You're not scared are you?" Nizza looked up in surprise.

"Ah . . . no, it's just that the last secret doors I went through resulted in very unpleasant experiences."

"Well, you don't have to worry this time. It's perfectly safe. It's called the go-betweens. I've been through here countless times and never seen so much as a whizzer or a breakfast bug."

"A what?"

"Never mind, let's just go." Nizza turned a small glass knob and the panel slid into the wall, revealing a space which looked like a very narrow hallway going off in three directions. "This is a junction," Nizza explained. "It's a place which connects two or more rooms. The narrow halls are called go-betweens because they are hidden between rooms."

The new sisters stepped into the hallway and Nizza slowly slid the panel closed. It became dark as the light from the music room diminished and then was shut off completely. Krystin could feel her old fears rising. "How will we see anything? You did bring a light, didn't you?"

The words were barely out of her mouth when a small blue light appeared. Krystin gasped, marveling at the light which was coming from a strange object in Nizza's hand. "What is that? How did you make it glow like that? Is it your magic?"

"This is just a fossi-shell," Nizza stated. "Nothing special."

"Nothing special? That's the most marvelous thing I've seen!"

"You mean you don't have these in Lyndell?"

"I have never even seen a . . . a . . . ," Krystin started.

"Shell?" Nizza finished.

"Yes, a shell, let alone one which shines. Is that magic?"

"No. Fossi-shells are found in the very deep sea. They are made by fossi-snails which leave their phosphorescence behind when they die. The am'Orans use them for light in their undersea caves, and for trade, after the snail dies or they eat them."

"But how do you make it shine?" Krystin asked.

"It is very cold in the deep seas. If I keep the shell warm in my hand or pocket, it is like any other shell I might find on the sand. If I hold it out and let it cool, it will begin to glow. The colder it gets the brighter it glows."

"Fascinating!" whispered Krystin. "Do you think I could get one?"

"Sure!" Nizza said. "You do have a lot to learn, don't you."

"Yes, I really do," Krystin admitted.

"No time to waste then!"

Nizza started down the center go-between at a fast pace with her new sister trailing behind her. There was only enough room for one person at a time. The walls were rough and unfinished looking, but the floor was level and smooth.

They came to another junction and Nizza turned right. At the next junction, they turned left and after ten paces, the younger sister came to a sudden stop. Krystin nearly fell over her trying to stop herself.

"What's the matter?" Krystin asked. "Where are we?"

"We must be very quiet from here on," Nizza whispered.

"Why?"

"You'll see when we get there."

The girls continued more slowly and in complete silence. Nizza took another right and then, putting her finger to her lips, motioned Krystin closer. As Krystin watched, Nizza slid back a tiny panel at eye level. At once they could hear voices. Nizza stepped to the side so her sister could see through the opening. There was some sort of material over the slit so it wasn't completely open to the other side of the wall. She could see in, but would not be seen.

The crown matriarch peered into the large, lavishly decorated room where several men sat around an oval table. The table was so large she could not see the ends on either side. She could not guess where it ended or how many people were actually seated there. Krystin's eyes took in the huge paintings that covered the wall she was facing. There were scenes of battles, both land and sea, portraits of noble men and women, and breathtaking landscapes, most strange and unfamiliar. The voices in the room were soft and murmuring. She could only make out a few words clearly.

The new matriarch was thinking she would like spy slits like this in Lyndell's castle, when suddenly she jumped at the loud mention of her name from the other room. She now focused her attention on what was actually being said and who was saying it.

". . . and as you can see," the voice was saying, ". . . the very fact you have married this off-worlder and proceeded to have children without the consent of your future realm, has caused a major uprising." There was a murmur of many voices.

"The fact remains, councilors," stated a voice trying to be heard above the rest, "that is what I have done and I'm not willing to change it. I had my parents' blessing and that's all I felt I needed. If my mother was not excused for her period of mourning, I am confident she would speak to this issue in my wife's behalf."

Krystin drew in a quick breath as she recognized Merrick's strong voice, though she could not see him.

"But what about the blood-line, High Patriarch!" a third man spoke up. "Surely you understand the threat to the ruling patriarchal line."

"Yes, yes, Patriarch Pepperton, I quite understand," Merrick threw back. "But I don't think this is the crisis you make it out to be."

"High Patriarch!" a voice called from the right side.

"Patriarch Degler, Realm High Keeper of the Peace is recognized," called out a small man seated at the table directly across the room from where Krystin and Nizza stood concealed.

"That's Patriarch Timmen, the scribe," whispered Nizza. The other man who was standing mumbled and sat down.

"Patriarch Degler! You may speak," declared Merrick.

A tall, heavily built man stood, his back to the spy slit. He quietly looked around the oval table at the face of each person on the High Council of en'Edlia before he spoke with a deep, mellow voice.

"High Patriarch . . . members of the council," Degler began formally. "We have all witnessed the people's reaction to our new crown matriarch. They are not united in their determinations. One faction is curious and watchful, willing to wait to see how she will handle herself and the affairs of the realm. These are no threat. Another faction is wary, cautious and suspicious of any off-worlders. They can be dealt with and usually pose no immediate threats. The third group however is a grave concern. They have rallied around a rebellious group which call themselves the Xens. They have taken up the cry 'No M.O.W.s', meaning 'No Magicless, Off-Worlders'. This group is on the verge of violence and is actively recruiting those dealing in the dark magics. The core leaders have gone into hiding and I'm afraid, High Patriarch, they cannot be reasoned with."

"We witnessed some violence against us in the coach as we arrived. What have you done so far?" Merrick questioned him.

"I have posted extra guards at the palace. We rounded up as many as I can charge with conspiracy and imprisoned them. We also have threatened anyone who seemed remotely associated the Xens to disband and present their concerns peacefully through the laws of the realm."

"Well done, Degler. Thank you for your good judgment and support. Which I will need from each of you," the high patriarch raised his voice pointedly, ". . . if we are to get through this without a civil war."

Degler bowed to his leader and sat down, as the murmuring around the table began anew.

Krystin stepped away from the open slit, her face pale. "Get me out of here," she whispered, her eyes wide and glassy.

Nizza bit her lip as she quickly closed the slider. She was supposed to be helping her new sister feel at home, but now she really had, as her mother would say, "drug in the seaweed." That meant only one thing. A big stink! Or in other words, trouble.

CHAPTER 8

"**N**izzarian!"

Someone was calling her proper name. That was not good. Nizza cringed in her room as the call came formally outside her door with added emphasis. "Heiress of the Realm, Nizzarian! You are ordered to the presence of the high patriarch at once!"

Nizza dragged her feet as she trudged down the long corridors, up wide staircases, and through the twists and turns it took to reach the personal chambers of the high patriarch. All the way there she thought about her new sister. How she had let her down and how angry her brother was going to be.

Now she stood trembling before the huge, handsomely carved, double wooden doors. Last time she had been called here, her father was waiting behind the doors. He had been glad to see her. She doubted this time the person behind the doors would be in a happy mood.

Nervously, Nizza raised her hand to knock, but instead let her fingers fall gently on the carving. The relief was a beautiful seashell with wings, the emblem of en'Edlia. She let her fingers glide over the smooth, flowing lines. It felt comforting in a way.

She stopped suddenly as memories of her father flooded over her. How she missed him! He had been the strength of the family. He had been the heart of the family. It was hard realizing he was not there behind the doors now.

She remembered when she was younger, she would scamper away to this door to escape her strict teacher, or her stitchery, or her bath. She would knock twice, wait, then knock once more. It was her secret knock. From the other side of the door would come one knock, a pause, then two knocks. That was Father's secret answer. Then he would squeak open the door ever so slightly and say in his deepest voice, "Who dares disturb the King of the Sea Trolls?"

Her answer would always be, "It is I, the Maiden of the Sea! Let me in and I'll give you a kiss!" This was always fun and frightening at the same time. Nizza smiled inwardly and shivered at the remembered thrill.

Then the door would slowly open and Nizza would walk in. Her father would jump from behind the door, growling loudly. She knew he was there, but she always cried out just a bit anyway. Then she would run into his arms, give him a kiss on the cheek, just above his scratchy beard, while he swung her around laughing.

Nizza's eyes misted over with tears. She took a step back from those doors. She wiped her eyes on her sleeve and when she looked up, one door was slightly ajar. She gasped, venturing forward, somehow hoping beyond hope her father was still behind the door waiting for her.

As she reached for the door, it suddenly flew wide open. She was nearly knocked down by the oracle leaving the room with his apprentice, Emija, and Merrick right behind them.

Ardloh, in his flowing, dark green robes stood even taller than Merrick. The robe's edges were all embroidered with gold and white runes in the language of the first Irthians known to have come to the planet eons ago. The oracle's hood lay bunched on his broad shoulders and back. His sparse white hair stood out from his head as if electrified, and his pale-blue eyes were piercing under his bushy white brows. His face was lined and weathered, his nose adding a pointed exclamation to his face. Nizza thought him ancient, but he was certainly not frail.

"Ah, there you are!" Merrick said none too kindly to his sister. "I was about to send out Commander Arreshi to bring you in. I know you can't escape from her!" He looked down at Nizza, his dark eyes boring through her.

"Now, Merrick, don't be too hard on her," the oracle intervened. "Everyone here has been through quite a bit in the last few weeks." He smiled at Nizza and patted her shoulder. "And Nizza," he continued, "don't you be too hard on your brother. He's only been high patriarch a short time and he has much to learn." The aged man patted Merrick on the shoulder. His gaze intensified for a moment, then smiling at them both, he nodded and muttered, "Yes, yes, we shall see. Storms ahead, much to come." He turned then, just shuffling away, humming a strange tune.

"Good luck!" Emija whispered to Nizza, following after Ardloh.

Merrick and Nizza stood looking after them until they turned a corner and were out of sight. She turned to look at her brother. "What did Ardloh tell you?" she asked. He shrugged, and then motioned for her to come in.

The high patriarch's quarters were immense. Nizza's quarters would fit inside the sitting area with plenty of room to spare. High domed ceilings, dripping with coral chandeliers, crowned the lavishly painted walls which were hung with dozens of portraits of past leaders and important events in the history of en'Edlia. There were ships battling on the stormy seas; the members of the first high council; the signing of trade agreements with foreign ambassadors, and many others. Nizza loved the excitement she felt when gazing at these marvelous scenes. She loved en'Edlia.

The furniture was upholstered in smooth emerald-green silk and trimmed with gold braid and tassels. A wall-sized reflecting-glass dominated one end of the sitting room. The opposite wall had two huge doors, one opened to a dining room, and the other, a hallway which led to two bedrooms, a bathing room, private study, and several closets.

Nizza knew there were more than twenty pillows around in the chairs and group seating. It had been one of her games with Father to see how many they could stack up before the soft tower tumbled down around them.

However, Nizza was not here for games this time. She plopped into a deep cushioned chair where she slouched down trying to look small and innocent.

Merrick was pacing. How he reminded her of Father! The same heavy brows crashing together over his black, bottomless eyes. The same long stride with hands clutched behind his back. Nizza hoped he would have Father's compassion as well.

"Nizzarian . . ." Merrick began gruffly, but as his sister looked up into his face, he softened and sighed. "Nizza," he said more gently, kneeling down in front of her.

"I'm really concerned about Krystin. She's been very moody and quiet for several days now. She barely speaks to me or anyone else. I found her crying this morning. Do you know what's going on?"

Squirming in her seat, Nizza tried to think of what to say. Merrick would probably be angry if he found out she had been spying on the high council meeting. Not only that, but exposing Krystin to the true feelings of many of her new subjects had been quite an unexpected shock for the new matriarch.

"Well?" her brother prodded.

"Do you promise you won't get mad at me?"

"What?"

"You have to promise you won't get mad at me."

"Don't be ridiculous, Nizza!"

"Promise! Or I'm not telling you anything."

"Oh, all right," he said standing. "I promise. But I'll have you know it is treason holding back information from the high patriarch!"

"Pledge the truth or you'll kiss a slime slug?"

"Nizza, we haven't done that since we were little!"

"I know, but it's the strongest promise-binding I know."

Merrick sighed and slowly put his hand over his heart. "I pledge the truth or I'll kiss a slime slug. There! Are you satisfied now?"

Still nervous, Nizza nodded, then slouched down in the chair even further.

"Well? Get on with it! Tell me what you know," cried Merrick in frustration as he sat on the edge of a chair facing her.

Nizza frowned at him. "You promised not to get mad."

"I'm not mad," he lowered his voice. "Just very concerned about my wife. Please, Nizza."

His sister sat up straight, trying to look confident. "It all started when I was showing my dear, new sister around the go-betweens. We just happened to be passing by the high council room when . . . ."

"You didn't!"

"Well . . . sort of," Nizza hunched her shoulders.

"What did she hear?"

"Um . . ."

"Nizza . . . tell me!"

"Um, she . . . she heard all about the different groups which don't like the fact you married her and all the trouble it's causing in en'Edlia," Nizza blurted.

She squeezed her eyes shut and covered her head with a pillow. After several seconds went by and she had heard no sound, she slowly uncovered her eyes and looked over at Merrick.

Merrick took the news like a punch in the stomach. His head in his hands, a single tear dropped to the floor.

Nizza was gripped with guilt. She quickly moved to kneel in front of her brother and, placing her hands on him, she began to use her birth-gift to ease his pain.

After a few seconds, her brother looked up into her face. "What shall we do?" he wondered. His face was pale and scrunched up with emotion. "Oh, Nizza, I love her so. How can I protect her in this terrible situation I have brought her into? You have to help me."

"I'm trying to," whispered Nizza meekly, increasing the outpouring of her gift.

"I don't mean help me," Merrick said, taking Nizza's hands off him. "I mean help me help Krystin."

"Oh." Nizza sat back on her heels, and then scooted back into the more comfortable chair. The room was silent as the two siblings thought. Nizza thought about how she would feel if she were Krystin. She knew a great deal about her new sister now that they had spent so much time together. She had been thrilled at the stories Krystin told her about life in Lyndell and her adventures with her brother, David. They hadn't lived like royalty when they were young. Still, Krystin had learned some things in all her growing up years which could certainly help her now.

"Merrick," Nizza suddenly said, sitting up excitedly. "Why do you think you need to protect Krystin from everything?"

Her brother looked confused as he brushed his sleeve over his face. "What do you mean?" he demanded. "Don't you think she needs protection?"

"Yes, and no."

"Listen, Nizza, when it comes to matters of state . . ." the high patriarch began.

"Hear me out," Nizza interrupted him. "I may be young and inexperienced in matters of state, as you say, but I happen to know your wife is the bravest woman I know besides our own mother."

"But . . ."

"I'm not finished," Nizza stated and then continued. "Krystin has faced a dragon and tamed it. She has befriended a swamp monster. She faced down the wizard, Zarcon and persuaded her older brother to come with her. She is willing to take chances to help those she loves, and . . ." Nizza paused looking pointedly at her brother. ". . . she enchanted you."

"I know all that," Merrick said, his face coloring slightly. "What's your point?"

"The fact is, if my sister is crown matriarch now and someday high matriarch, she is going to have to show the people she can do it. Stand up for her right to be here now. Think about how strong Mother is. Krystin is going to have to face them, persuade them, befriend them, help them, take chances, love them and enchant them."

"Just like she did with me," Merrick said softly, with a faraway look in his dark eyes.

"Yes, just like she did with you," Nizza nodded.

Merrick sat back, looking at the high ceiling for several minutes. Nizza was content to let him think about what she had said as she curled up in the chair thinking her own thoughts.

She gazed at her brother wondering if he would even consider what she had said. Slowly she saw a change come over his face and then he smiled.

"You know, Nizza," he said as he sat forward setting his deep-dark eyes upon her. "I just may have to have you counsel me more often on 'matters of state'!" He laughed and moved to hug her.

Nizza hugged her brother as tears clouded her eyes. Her brother seemed so like her father at that moment. She missed his warm hugs, strong arms and love.

"I think you may have just come up with the most marvelous idea," Merrick said as he held her at arm's length and smiled broadly. "Let's do some planning right now on how to implement this idea starting tomorrow!"

"The sooner the better!" agreed Nizza, feeling happy and relieved.

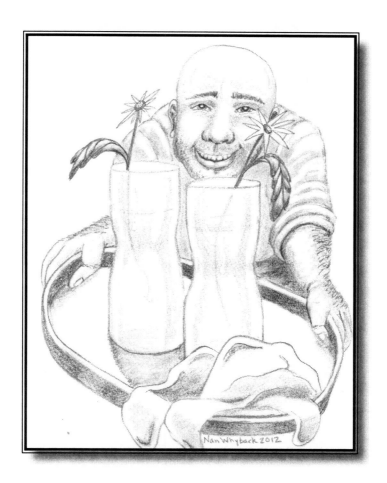

CHAPTER 9

Nizza was pink with excitement. After arranging for Leesel to care for the twins, she and Krystin were on their way to the center of the city. Of course there was a large group of palace guards a few paces behind them. If she didn't look back, it felt like she and her sister were all alone, out for a day of fun in the market place.

Merrick had insisted upon the guards and a certain amount of casual disguise for Krystin and Nizza. No pomp and ceremony, just plain clothes and light, hooded cloaks. Nothing to announce, "Here is the crown matriarch!"

Nizza had argued that the crowd of guards would be just such an announcement, so Merrick had ordered the guard to dress down, mingle with the people and keep a respectful distance. Nevertheless, he was still very worried.

So far, the plan was a success. Krystin was pleased with the plan, even though she was feeling apprehensive about going out amongst the people who didn't want her in en'Edlia. However, they were now her people too. She had to face them and try to learn their ways to be a part of them.

Smells of fish, spices, and flowers mingled together into a wonderful aroma long before the market came into sight. Sounds of eager customers haggling over prices, sellers calling out the wonders of their wares, children laughing, and the constant cries of the sea birds created a symphony of sounds.

Nizza loved this place. She glanced over at Krystin's face to see if she was feeling as excited. Krystin suddenly clutched Nizza's hand as her eyes grew large. Feeling the cool moistness of her sister's hand, Nizza could tell Krystin was not feeling the same excitement she was. She realized Krystin was frightened. *How could she have not remembered!* Krystin had been overwhelmed with the huge crowds the first day. She had not really been out of the palace since. Of course she'd be nervous, even scared in such a situation. Nizza needed to change the plan.

Taking her sister's trembling arm, Nizza steered her to the right, down an alleyway, and on into a quieter part of the city. Here were small shops and streets full of children and their pets playing. Homes lined many parts of the streets, along with shade trees, and giant flowering bushes.

"Nizza!" Krystin cried, gripping her new sister even tighter. "Where are we going?"

Nizza nervously glanced behind them. The guards were noticeably confused by her change of direction and some were even trying to catch up to them. She frowned and waved them back.

"You'll see," she smiled tensely up at Krystin. "Just a little change in plans."

"But, the guards! And Merrick! What will they say?"

"Don't worry. It will be fine. You'll see."

Coming to a small eating park, Nizza guided Krystin to a seat and sat next to her. A server bustled up to them, smiling.

"Good day, lovely women!" he called out cheerfully. He was a large round man, sweating slightly in the warm sun. He had huge white teeth which he flashed at them like a trophy. "How may this humble servant help you?"

"Two ichy-fruit drinks, please," Nizza replied smiling back. "And can you add a little extra zulijiuce, please?"

"For you, my little radiant flower, anything!" beamed the server as he scurried away.

"Do you know him?" Krystin asked.

"No, why?"

"He seemed very friendly. I thought maybe you knew him."

"No, that's just the way people are in this part of the city."

"I thought we were going to the market?"

"Well, you looked very anxious, so I thought it might be better to start small and work up to the market."

"Oh. I see." Krystin blushed and looked down.

"You're not disappointed, are you? We can always go back." Nizza looked at Krystin's downcast face trying to read her emotions.

"No. You're right." Krystin gave Nizza a sad smile. "I am nervous."

Nizza sighed with relief and placed a hand on her sister's arm, letting her birth-gift flow into Krystin. "It's all right. Just pretend you are at home in Lyndell. Be yourself. Be happy. Smile. Talk to the people. Ask them questions."

"I feel so overwhelmed. It's like I don't even know the language here."

Nizza laughed. "It will get better. Remember the things we talked about before. I'll help you!"

"I know you will. You have already helped me so much." Krystin patted Nizza's hand knowing she was feeling that warm, happy feeling from her sister.

Nizza blushed. "Well, except for one time in the go-betweens."

Krystin took Nizza's hand. "I'm even glad about that, Nizza. I needed to know. It's been hard, but now that I know, I can do something about it."

A strong-looking woman approached and sat at another table near them.

"Warm day, isn't it?" she said casually.

"Yes," replied Nizza without looking at her. "Warm day."

Krystin recognized the woman as Commander Arreshi, the one who could generate a force field. She felt herself relax a bit as an idea popped into her head. "Tell me, good matriarch," Krystin began addressing Arreshi, raising her voice and smiling slightly. "Have you seen anything of the crown matriarch? I hear she's a witch!"

The commander looked shocked, not knowing what to say. "I . . . I . . . well, I . . ."

Nizza caught Krystin's grin at her and joined in the fun at the commander's expense. "Yes, good woman, tell us! Need we be wary of this off-worlder?"

There were several other people sitting around who now became very interested in this new conversation.

"No need to fear," Krystin continued, as she winked at Arreshi and then looked around at the others in the outdoor-eating seats. "We are all friends here."

Nizza noticed many heads nodding. She smiled at Krystin's cleverness. The commander, more used to being on guard than being in the social spotlight, finally pulled herself together and spoke up.

"I have seen the crown matriarch," she began. Then lowering her voice for effect, she nearly whispered, "But she's no witch! She was very kind to me and my companions. And . . . ." She paused to see if everyone was indeed listening, which they were very intently. "She's very beautiful as well!" she said and winked at Nizza.

Just then the server returned whistling as he set their drinks in front of them.

"Will there be anything else, my fragrant flowers?" he asked, bowing low.

"Yes, handsome sir," said Krystin confidently. "We would like some muffybread if you please, and a small cup of razor fish liver paste on the side." She smiled at him warmly. "Thank you for your most excellent service!"

The server stood up straight and gave them an even larger smile, his pride nearly bursting through his shirt front.

"I am your slave," he gushed, bowing so low his hand brushed the ground.

He turned smartly on his heels, nearly running to fulfill their desires.

As soon as he was gone the two sisters could barely contain their giggling. Then they turned to Arreshi, who was already ambling away toward the rest of the guard, smiling knowingly.

There were excited conversations all around them now as the new information about the crown matriarch flooded from mouths to ears.

The rest of the day was wonderful as they drifted in and out of the small shops, stopping here and there to talk with shop keepers or city people. Each time making unkind comments about the new crown matriarch which were quickly, yet quietly refuted by one of the guards who took turns playing the part of an innocent bystander. By the time the two sisters found their way back to the palace, they were laughing with happy exhaustion.

At the news of their return, Merrick hurried to find them. They were sprawled in the high patriarch's quarters with their eyes closed and smiles on their faces.

"Well?" he demanded as he stormed into the room. "What happened? The palace guards would tell me nothing! Are you all right?"

The sisters sat up then, looked at each other and burst out laughing.

"What?" Merrick cried. "Are you going to tell me?" He gazed into their sparkling eyes and mischievous smiles. "Or do I have to tickle it out of you!" He crouched down, curling his wiggling fingers as he slowly advanced toward them.

"Oh, no!" cried both sisters together, as they edged away.

"Please, no, Merrick!" pleaded his wife. "I don't have the strength!"

"We've had a miraculous day, dear brother!" admitted Nizza. "Our plan is working!"

"Really?" questioned Merrick, amazed, as he sat down next to Krystin and put his arm around her. "I was so worried the whole time you were gone."

"Well . . . ." started Krystin, "you needn't have been since you sent half an army with us."

"It didn't go exactly as we planned," Nizza cut in, "but close enough."

She and Krystin took turns telling him all about the change in plans and how the day had gone.

"We kind of made it up as we went, the guards joined in, and it all worked out just fine," Nizza concluded.

"No wonder the guards wouldn't tell me," Merrick grinned. "They probably thought they had too much fun and not enough duty, by the sound of it." Merrick sat quietly for a moment, then said, "But no one knew who you were? No one recognized you?"

"I'm not sure about me," answered Nizza. "Some may have guessed. When we left each place we left one of these behind." She handed her brother a small piece of cloth with the crest of en'Edlia painted on it. "That way they might not know while we were there, but could figure it out later, once we were safely away."

Merrick just shook his head and grinned. "Well, I should have guessed you two together were smart enough to figure things out. You are amazing!" He drew both of them into his arms.

"Now," said Nizza seriously, sitting back down and looking from the high patriarch to the crown matriarch. "Now to begin part two of the plan!"

CHAPTER 10

The next several days were spent indoors as a storm blew in from the sea. High winds tossed the ships in the harbor, while waves pounded the shores. Black clouds blanketed the skies and rain poured down flooding the streets. The market square cleared out as merchants closed their tents, covering their precious wares against the wind-driven rain. The eating parks were deserted except for the occasional snuffler or small groups of long-tailed scurriers, scavenging for scraps of food.

Nizza and Krystin sat opposite each other playing a game of Shells on a highly polished wooden board. Meanwhile, Wayen was busy in his own quarters getting Smich into some dry clothes because he had sneaked to the palace against his mother's wishes again.

The high matriarch sat near the window watching the black clouds pour out their contents as they rumbled and bumped across the sky. She had her needlework in her hands. The needle slowly moved, on its own, through the fabric, drawing the thread into intricate patterns on the cloth. She used her birth-gift in so few things but this was one she enjoyed.

Nizza glanced up at her mother's still figure fearing she may be crying. Instead she saw a small smile on her lips and peace in her eyes. She saw the embroidery needle moving and smiled. Her mother hadn't sewn a stitch since Father had died. It was a good sign.

"Mother?" Nizza said softly. "What are you thinking about?"

Narrian continued to gaze out the window. "Your father loved the storms of the sea." she said wistfully. "He said they were wild and untamable. He loved the feeling of their power. It made him feel small and humble."

The high matriarch turned now to look at her daughters as she continued. "I was remembering a time when your father and I were sailing home from po'Enay. We were there on a diplomatic mission before you were born. A fierce storm came up lasting three days. The sea was extremely rough. Many of the crew were frightened and could barely perform their duties.

"But not your father. High patriarch or not, he rolled up his regal sleeves and set to work helping with the ship's rigging. He worked alongside the crew, encouraging them, taking orders from the captain just like the rest. He gained many blisters on that trip, along with many loyal followers. There is much to be said for being among the people as one of them, instead of standing above them." She smiled at her daughters now.

"You are so wise for ones so young," she told them. "Merrick indeed chose wisely when he chose you, Krystin. And Nizza, my only daughter until now. So much like your father, you are Nizza. Brave and a bit reckless. I'm proud of you both."

Krystin blushed under Narrian's praise while Nizza beamed, taking her sister's hand. "And just wait until this storm clears!" said Nizza confidently. "We will be among the people again."

* * *

The weather had given Nizza a few extra days to think her plans through and talk more with Krystin about it. Just last night, Nizza had had the dream again about the strange new tower rising up and being attacked by an angry storm. She woke sweating in the night, breathing hard and shaking. As Nizza had lain in her bed listening to the distant thunder of the retreating storm, she tried to tell herself it was just a dream. Nevertheless, she couldn't shake the foreboding feeling it had left inside her.

The storm at last blew itself away over the mountains after four long days. The sun began its labor of drying up the puddled streets, sodden grass and dampened spirits of en'Edlia. It was time for the second part of Nizza's plan to begin. Today they would enter the grand market place in the main square. There would be hundreds of people out and about, buying and selling, gawking and gossiping, strolling and sunning after the storm. It would be the perfect day.

The steamy sidewalks eagerly let go of the remaining moisture. The flower borders raised their drooping heads to feel the sun's warmth. The sisters were excited though a bit nervous, but that made it all the more thrilling. They were on their way to the city's center market with smiles on their faces and heads held high. They chatted about what they would do when they reached the market, the palace guard again trailing in plain clothes at a respectful distance.

Suddenly a figure appeared directly in front of them, blotting out the sun momentarily. The girls came to an abrupt halt to avoid colliding with the figure.

Krystin jumped and clutched at Nizza as she looked up at the tall figure, whose face was concealed in the shadow of a dark, hooded cloak.

Nizza, squinting in the bright light, tried to make out the face. Before she could say anything, he spoke.

"Beware this sunlit path you take, for it may bring a storm of greater fury than we have yet seen these past four days."

His deep, ominous voice was quiet, yet Nizza felt it pierce her soul. Again the memory of her dream surfaced and she shuddered. She realized then it was the oracle. "Ardloh!" Nizza cried. "You startled us!"

"And that was my intent," the oracle replied gently. "Take my warning to heart, young heiress. Perhaps today is not as bright as it appears."

Nizza frowned. Ardloh had been around forever it seemed, or at least as long as she could remember. He always spoke in strange ways, sometimes like a puzzle that was missing a piece. She had never really spoken with him personally before. Now here he was jumping into her plans and trying to scare them.

"What do you mean?" Krystin spoke up then, her voice filled with concern. "Is there another storm coming?" She glanced up into the cloudless sky as a passing seabird shrieked.

"Even the birds know," said Ardloh cryptically, glancing up as well.

"Oh, Ardloh," laughed Nizza. "The sky is clear. We are just going to the market. We will have plenty of time to get back to the palace before it will rain again."

Perhaps it is a good thing, thought Nizza, *that Ardloh is training his new apprentice, Emija, to take his place. He seems to be growing senile after all these years.* She decided to change the subject.

"How is Emija doing with her training, Ardloh?"

The oracle just stared at her for several moments. Nizza was about to repeat her question, a little louder this time, when he suddenly threw back his hood, glaring at her sternly.

Nizza gasped, stepping back. Ardloh's sparse white hair glowed in the sun and created a halo effect around his head. His bright blue eyes seemed to have a light of their own.

"You are smart, Nizzarian, but beware nonetheless. I am aged, but my mind is clear and sees beyond what can be seen. Storms can rage in many ways. Can you not feel it within you even now?"

She did feel it. The dream. Her emotions churned inside her. She couldn't think clearly as Ardloh looked at her so intently.

"What is it, Nizza?" Krystin touched Nizza's arm causing her to turn, breaking the eye contact with the oracle.

"Huh? What?" Nizza muttered.

"Nizza?" Krystin said again.

"Do not worry, Krystin," said Ardloh, turning his gaze upon her. She is well enough. Nizza has a good spirit like her father, but is young and a bit reckless."

Krystin looked down, blushing at Ardloh's attention.

Just then Arreshi, Commander of the Palace Guard arrived, looking very concerned. "Is there a problem, Great Oracle?" she questioned, glancing around warily.

Ardloh frowned at the use of his title. "Good day, Commander," he said gently. "There is no cause for immediate alarm. See well to your duties though. All is not well in en'Edlia, but better days will come." Instantly he vanished.

They all stood around looking puzzled for several moments. Finally Krystin asked, "Well, are we still going to the market or not?"

Krystin looked at Arreshi, who looked at Nizza, who stood staring at the place where Ardloh had been a moment before.

Nizza's thoughts and feelings were in a whirl. *What should I do now? Why did Ardloh have to interfere with my plans? And for what? The threat of rain sometime in the future?* Again her thoughts went back to her dream. *And how did he know so much about that? What does my dream mean? How does it connect with what we are doing now?*

Finally, she stomped her foot. She had a plan and she was going through with it.

"Yes!" She said to no one in particular. "We are going! And going right now!"

CHAPTER 11

The small group entered the grand market place practically unnoticed. The streets were thronged with eager shoppers, restless children, and those looking for a diversion after being cooped up for days during the storm. Numerous animals, slinking underfoot and in shadowy corners, joined them.

Few noticed the many smaller groups of plain-clothed guards which followed the first group at a respectful, but watchful distance.

Even Nizza's step wasn't as springy and carefree as it had been when they had left the palace that morning. *That Ardloh!* she thought bitterly. *Casting his gloom over our bright dreams like an unwelcomed rain cloud passing over the sun on the day of a long-awaited picnic.* Now the whole company was spooked like a hordle in a swarm of slappers.

Krystin gasped as she glanced around the buzzing market place. The sights and sounds which were so familiar to Nizza were breathtaking to her. Colorful long-tailed birds squawked in hanging cages; small furry animals skittered about in wooden crates; spices and herbs gave the air a rich, pungent odor combined with the delicious aromas of fruits and earthy vegetables piled high; ornate containers of bright jewelry flashed in the sunlight; bolts of colorful fabrics were stacked higher than their heads; woven carpets, garments, shoes, and so much more were an ever-changing feast for the senses. Krystin wanted to take it all in.

Their misgivings were soon forgotten in the excitement of the grand market shops. "Look at this!" Krystin cried, pointing to a tiny, long-tailed animal with bulging eyes clinging to the fingers of its owner.

"This little gem can be yours, sweet miss," whispered the seller, ". . . for the lowly price of three pa'trees!" Nizza shook her head. "I'll throw in a week's food for free!" the owner called after them as Nizza steered Krystin away.

"Oh, Nizza!" The crown matriarch had stopped at yet another stall. "This is so beautiful!" Krystin's eyes shone as she fingered some fine silken fabric imported from across the seas. It was woven through with a rainbow of colored threads making such an intricate pattern, that Krystin could not fathom how it was done. It was so light and gauzy and smooth to the touch.

"For you, my amber flower," called the short, fat merchant to Krystin, "a special price! Only ten pa'trees a length! Only for the next few moments!" he smiled broadly.

"Can we buy anything?" whispered Krystin to Nizza frantically.

"Better not spend much or we'll raise some attention," her sister whispered back. "We can have the servants come and get some of that material later if you really like it."

"What fun is going to the marketplace if you can't buy anything?" Krystin questioned, smiling. Nevertheless, she was just happy to be there.

Suddenly there was a great musical crashing ahead of them as brightly dressed callers came through the crowds announcing the next performance of the Great Bafoolee and his Amazing Puppets at the center-square stage just a few blocks away. Krystin squeaked with excitement as she bounced up and down begging Nizza to go with her. Nizza shrugged and was promptly pulled, half running, half stumbling, the three blocks to the market square where a huge crowd was gathering for Bafoolee's next performance.

On a raised platform in a small park, just to the right of the main road through the grand market square, there was a large stage front with satin curtains of red and gold surrounded by a large framework of carved wood. Gems and mirrors embedded in the wood caught the sunshine, glittering like flashing lights. Children pushed to the front amid complaining adults, who hid their smiles remembering their own youthful excitement. There was an air of adventure as the music of the callers came back around until they stood in front of the stage playing nonsensical tunes on drums, flutes and cymbals.

On an unseen cue, the music suddenly stopped, the musicians filed off. The curtains of the stage opened to the gasping crowd. There, before their eyes, were life-sized puppets, painted and jointed to move like living persons. They were made of all sorts of materials like animal fur, bones, wood, and shells. The puppets stood perfectly still and the audience held their breath waiting for the action to begin.

A loud, musical crash made everyone jump as one of the puppets came to life.

"Welcome, I am The Great Bafoolee!" it announced. "These are my amazing puppets!" The audience oohed and aahed.

"But, you may say, I am only a puppet myself!"

"Yes, yes!" cried the audience.

"Then you would be mistaken!" it announced. Stepping off the stage, its puppet-like features melted away and a real man stood before them. Everyone burst into applause.

"And now for our performance!" shouted Bafoolee. The music began again and the puppets came to life moving on their own, performing a hilarious comedy routine.

Krystin was mystified. *How was it done?* Nizza nudged her, pointing to Bafoolee standing on the side moving his hands and magically controlling the puppets with his birth-gift. Even the children seemed to know all about it, but didn't care in the least. They laughed and clapped and swayed to the music during the whole show.

Krystin clapped until her hands hurt. Tears of laughter wet her cheeks. What a wonderful thing! She had never seen puppets on such a large scale in Lyndell.

Once again Bafoolee stepped to the front of the stage.

"Many thanks to all of you for your kind attention!" called out the puppet master. "Please show your happiness by adding your coins to my small coffers." The musicians walked through the crowd with boxes, collecting a few coins from their audience. "And now if you have any questions for any of my puppets . . . ." he paused expectantly, bowing low.

The crowd began to murmur and disperse, seeing the main excitement was over. Krystin pushed forward, intrigued by Bafoolee's invitation.

"Come, come, ladies and gentlemen!" he beckoned after his retreating audience. "Surely you would ask The Great Bafoolee a question or two?"

Krystin looked at Nizza, smiling. "What about it?" she asked. "We are here for exposure, right?"

Nizza felt unsure, hanging back. Kristin threw up her hand and called out, "I have a question!"

The puppet master's face lit up. "Aw, a brave one emerges," he said softly to himself. "Come forward, lovely lady!" he called aloud. "Ask what you will," he said bowing. Some people stayed thinking there might be more to see now someone had volunteered.

Standing in front of the stage, Krystin smiled and looked over the puppets. One puppet was dressed as a royal figure, like a king or prince. "What is his name?" she asked Bafoolee, pointed to the puppet.

"His name is Kneal," he replied gently. "For all kneel before him." He laughed at his own joke, then continued. "But surely that isn't your only question?" he asked, a small smile creasing his broad, face.

"Oh, no," replied Krystin. "I wanted to ask him what he thinks of the new crown matriarch."

Bafoolee laughed. "A brave question in these troubled times, lovely lady! But ask what you will." He bowed again, motioning to Kneal.

"Very well, Kneal," said Krystin seriously. "What do you think of the new crown matriarch?"

Kneal, the puppet, shuddered, coming to life. His movements were stiff and awkward as he took two steps forward then turned his head to look toward Krystin. His eyes were set with small, blue gems so they shone in the light. Kneal cocked his head to one side and then spoke.

"That is a very good question. One for which there are many answers," replied Kneal.

Krystin felt her skin prickle as the face of Kneal shifted and softened until he looked very, very human. It was unnerving and she edged back as he leaned closer to her.

"But for me," he continued, staring at her. "I think she is very beautiful, yet mysterious. I would fear for her safety in some circles."

Krystin shivered with the intensity of his words and the way he looked at her as if he could really see her.

Kneal kept talking. "I think she should make herself more known to the people of en'Edlia so they can judge more intelligently her intent and character."

Krystin gasped and blurted out, "But that's what I'm trying to do . . . ." She suddenly realized what she had revealed. She forgot he was only a puppet, being manipulated by someone else. He seemed so real. She quickly looked around her, feeling self-conscious.

Nizza came quickly to her side, not knowing what to expect next. She glanced around trying to see the guards among the crowd. There were still many people gathered around within hearing range. Most of those now turned toward Krystin, staring.

Kneal suddenly began yelling and waving his arms. "Come one, come all!" the puppet announced loudly. "See our great crown matriarch! Ask her what you will!" Kneal became very animated, dancing across the stage and waving his arms, his face like a puppet again, as Bafoolee grinned from the shadows.

"No . . . no . . . I didn't mean . . . , no, I'm not ready . . ." stammered Krystin as the crowd now turned toward her, pressing closer.

CHAPTER 12

Krystin stared at the crowd somewhat fearfully. *Isn't this what I came here for?* she asked herself. *Isn't this what I wanted? A chance to get to know the people and for the people to get to know me? Well, then, be brave, Krystin! No one here is breathing fire. At least not yet.*

"Are you really the crown matriarch?" asked a young boy right in front.

"Well, yes," Krystin replied timidly. "Yes, I'm Crown Matriarch Krystin, wife of High Patriarch Merrick." Just stating her title gave her courage.

"I'm Doogan," replied the boy. "Watch what I can do!" Doogan wrinkled his nose and squinted his eyes, then he began to fade slowly until he finally disappeared altogether. At Krystin's amazed gasp, he popped back into being.

"That was wonderful!" Krystin told him. Doogan beamed proudly. His mother stepped up behind him, placing a hand on his shoulder.

"That's enough, son. I'm sure the crown matriarch has more important questions to answer."

"It's all right," Krystin assured her. "That was amazing. You must be very proud of him." She smiled kindly as the woman nodded shyly.

"What can you do?" asked Doogan suddenly, tugging on her sleeve.

"Me?" Krystin said surprised. "I . . . well, I . . ." she stammered, her thoughts tumbling over and over. *What should I say? The truth. Always tell the truth.* "I once tamed a dragon even though I don't have any magical powers," she admitted. "But I know how to love and be kind.

"No magic?" Doogan looked at her sadly, then he smiled brightly. "Momma says just wait and it will come." He gently touched Krystin's arm, whispering, "Just wait and it will come."

The child waved as his mother pulled him away toward the other stalls to finish her shopping. "I like you even with no magic!" he called over his shoulder.

She looked up into the faces of the crowd which now surrounded her. *Just wait and it will come. Perhaps Doogan is right,* Krystin thought.

"Hello, everyone!" the crown matriarch greeted her new people more confidently. "What else would you like to know about me?"

"Do you have any sisters?" called out one young man from the back. Krystin blushed.

"Just my new sister-in-law, Nizza," she said smiling, inviting Nizza to stand next to her. The young man smiled back, glancing at Nizza as her face grew red.

A frizzy, red-haired woman spoke up brashly. "I heard your family killed everyone from our world who came to your world!"

"I'm sorry, but that is not true," Krystin stated matter-of-factly. "Zarcon was killed by a swamp monster when he tried to kill my brothers and me. Odethia was captured by Merrick and brought back here unharmed. Both were workers of dark magic and caused much grief on our world. The only other person from your world who came to my world, at least that I know, is High Patriarch Merrick, and I married him!" Krystin smiled broadly as some people laughed.

"What do you want to change here?" one woman called out.

"Change? Well, nothing . . ." started Krystin. "I think en'Edlia is a wonderful place."

"So you don't think anything should be done to correct some of our current problems?" a man said, his voice rising.

"Well, I didn't mean . . ."

"Would you want someone from our world as ruler of your world?" someone yelled from the back.

"Well, that depends," Krystin began. "Someone like Zarcon, no. But Merrick certainly helped my father, the King of Lyndell, when he was there, so . . ."

"So you're not involved with the Xens?"

"I'm not sure who they are."

"Are you for or against increasing trade involvement with King Raden Rex VIII?" someone asked quickly.

"I don't know who he is either. Could you . . ."

"What about your children?" another man asked, not even letting Krystin finish.

"My children?" Krystin replied, confused.

"Oh, your twins are so cute," a young mother with an infant in her arms suddenly said. "Are you planning to have more?"

"Thank you," responded Krystin, blushing at the personal question. "Yes, we would like to have more children."

"But do they show any signs of birth-gifts?" the same man continued, frowning at the young mother.

"I'm not sure. We haven't really . . ."

"There!" declared the man loudly, throwing up his arms as he turned to the crowd. "Are we willing to be ruled by magicless off-worlders? I say no!"

Krystin tried to speak up. "The twins are still very young and Merrick says . . ."

Murmuring rippled through the crowd which was now rapidly increasing in size. It had started with just a few dozen, but was now a few hundred and growing. Nizza could see the palace guards struggling to make their way to the front as they heard angry voices being raised. Her panic increased as some in the group began chanting, "No M.O.W.s! No M.O.W.s!"

"Please!" Krystin cried out determinedly. "Please, let's just talk about this." However, she couldn't be heard over the chanting and arguing that others had now taken up against the chanters.

Nizza grabbed Krystin's arm. "We have to get out of here!" Nizza told her as she began to use her birth-gift to soothe the growing hostility she was feeling from the crowd. There were too many people to calm everyone, but she might be able to reach the ones closest to them.

"No, wait," Krystin said gently but firmly, pushing off from Nizza and climbing up onto the stage.

"Good people of en'Edlia!" Crown Matriarch Krystin called out loudly. "Please hear me!"

"No M.O.W.s! **NO M.O.W.s!**" The chanting got louder.

"Give her a chance!" a voice cried out.

"The high patriarch had no right to do it!" said another.

"I want to hear what she has to say!"

"Don't listen to her! She's going to destroy our way of life!"

"Go back to your own world!"

Krystin yelled as loud as she could, trying to be heard, but the crowd's voices were intensifying as they began to break into opposing groups. She felt something whiz past her head.

Kneal, the puppet, came up beside her and began mocking her every move. Some in the crowd began to laugh and point. She felt humiliated being manipulated by a puppet! She cast an angry look at Bafoolee, who just frowned, making a gesture which closed the curtains of the stage behind her. He was not happy at the loss of business that day.

Nizza turned to the crowd begging them to stop, pleading in Krystin's behalf for them to listen. No one was paying any attention. The crowd began to press forward, swarming the stage. Hands were reaching out, pushing and shoving. The sisters couldn't stop them. The crowd was becoming a mob! Where were the guards? Why weren't they helping?

Nizza tried to reach her sister, to pull Krystin down from the stage, to move her toward the oncoming palace guards. Struggling to break free from the tightening group of people jostling around her, Nizza pushed out with her birth-gift, giving warmth and happiness to any who came near. It was of little use as the flow of people constantly changed. She found herself being pushed away from the stage as others crowded toward it.

Palace Guard Commander Arreshi was pushing with all her might to get close enough to the sisters to put a force-field of protection around them. Suddenly a hail of rocks came raining down from somewhere toward the back of the crowd. Several women screamed as the crowd began to stampede in all directions.

Before the commander could come within range to protect her, Krystin was struck several times. Wailing with hurt and shame and a deep sense of failure, Krystin collapsed just as Arreshi's field closed around her.

Nizza, caught in the waves of people, couldn't get to her sister. She cried out as she saw a trickle of blood appear on Krystin's forehead. Rough hands pushed Nizza from behind and she went down to the ground. Weak from using her gift so intensely, she couldn't get up and was soon battered by stomping feet and running legs.

The guards used their birth-gifts to push back the citizens and disperse the crowd. One amplified his voice and gave the announcement, "CLEAR THE AREA! DISPERSE PEACEABLY! BY ORDER OF THE PALACE GUARD!"

One telepathically called for reinforcements from the palace. Another became invisible, searching for those throwing rocks or causing damage, using a capturing stone to nab them.

Arreshi, shouting orders to her guards, caught a glimpse of Nizza, bruised and nearly unconscious on the ground. She instantly extended a second field around Nizza, checking on her condition.

Nizza saw the force field's blurry color form around her. Great tears welled up in her eyes. She lay hurting inside and outside. She felt so weak. *Where is Krystin?* she thought. *What have I done! My dream is coming true as Ardloh predicted. Krystin has been hurt because of my plan. We could have been killed!* There was a great throbbing in her head and her body ached all over. Her heart felt like it was being squeezed by iron hands. *Why was I so stubborn?* She felt herself losing consciousness. Darkness was closing in upon her mind. *Why didn't I listen to the oracle?*

A guard teleported back to the palace with both sisters. They were met by servants who hurried them inside to the palace physician's healing quarters. Other healers were called to the scene to treat those who had been injured when the once friendly crowd had turned ugly.

Commander Arreshi shook her head angrily as she watched the last of the people drift away. Something had gone terribly wrong today. She knew she would have to answer to the high patriarch for it.

CHAPTER 13

A week had passed since the riot in the en'Edlia city center. Most things in en'Edlia had returned to normal. Most people had found something else to talk about. Nizza was still confined to her room, spending time in quiet healing. Leesel and Boolie watched the twins in the nursery as

Merrick and Krystin strolled in the palace gardens alone. They came here often for quiet stolen moments of time together.

The gardens were renowned for their unique plant life and flowers created by Tesh, the palace gardener. His birth-gift was growing plants and changing them as he willed. His talent was envied by many and copied by none. The gardener had been part of Merrick's life for as long as he could remember. He and his brother, Jarrius often played in, on, and all around the expansive palace gardens, meticulously kept by Tesh alone.

As the couple passed the gardener, busy in his work, he bowed, and said humbly, "I am honored by your presence. May I show you my newest creation?"

The pair nodded graciously. Tesh beamed at them, motioning them toward a bright green bush covered with fist-sized flower buds.

"This is my newest creation for the gardens," Tesh bowed again. He gently cradled a bud in his hand and it magically opened, its dozen petals spiraling slowly outward.

Krystin marveled at the delicate golden-yellow bloom. Its throat was touched with a most piercing blue and speckled with pale reddish-brown freckles. A fragrance, light and sweet, floated out into the air around them.

"I call it 'Krystin'", the gardener remarked quietly as if sharing an intimate secret. His cheeks colored slightly as he bowed again. "It is in your honor, Crown Matriarch." He smiled at Krystin.

"It is the most beautiful thing I have ever seen!" she whispered, her eyes moistening with emotion. "Thank you!" She took his hand in hers. "Thank you," she said again, her voice choked with emotion.

"Well done, Tesh!" Merrick commented. "A perfect match for my beautiful wife." He clapped Tesh on the shoulder as he placed his other arm around Krystin. "Have some of those brought up to our room, old friend." He smiled broadly at the still grinning gardener. "Truly a marvelous creation!"

Tesh bowed as the couple moved away to resume their walk amongst his other creations. He called after Merrick "I must say the gardens are easier to tend now you boys aren't tearing things up all the time!"

Merrick laughed and waved. "Wait until our daughters grow up a bit!"

They meandered on, winding through the paths. Birdsong caught their ears as gentle aromas delighted their senses from the myriad of fantastic, colorful blossoms that surrounded them. Nevertheless, Krystin's thoughts were wandering more than her feet.

Merrick broke the silence between them. "I've been thinking."

Krystin took his hand and gazed up into his face, waiting for him to go on.

"I've been thinking about making the voyage to the Raden Islands myself instead of sending Matriarch Birkin this time."

"How long will you be gone?" Krystin asked anxiously, tightening her grip on his hand.

Merrick stopped walking and gently pulled his wife to a nearby bench to sit down. He held her hands and looked into her eyes. He said nothing for a very long moment.

Tears began to appear in Krystin's eyes as she imagined him leaving and being gone for weeks, even months again. She was beginning to understand the sacrifice she would have to make the rest of her life being married to the ruler of en'Edlia. His country's needs would come first most of the time. It was his job, his duty, his life, and the life of his beloved country, and even his world. She had to swallow her feelings, bow to the country's needs, and her husband's duties as well. After all, she was the crown matriarch, someday to be high matriarch.

Narrian was an excellent role model, but Krystin still had much to learn. She must learn to be in control of herself and to be in control of the situation. She had learned this all too well. Krystin thought of her own mother. The years of hard work she had spent at the forest cottage, the worry for her children, the transition, not once but twice, between there and the life of a queen at Lyndell. Krystin had not been a willing student in her youth. Yet now looking back, she realized the many sacrifices her mother had made in the name of duty to the crown.

Merrick, looking down at his wife, cleared his throat. However, Krystin spoke up first. Gaining control of her emotions with difficultly, she dared not look up at her husband.

"I know how important this voyage is for the good of en'Edlia, Merrick. The people are concerned about peaceful trade agreements with King Raden. It needs to be resolved. I know of no one else who could handle it better than you." She blinked away her tears and tried to steady her voice. "I'll be fine here." She forced a smile for him, finally glancing up. "We'll be fine. And no more jaunts into town without an official escort, I promise."

A smile started at the corner of Merrick's mouth and spread over his face like sunshine from behind a windswept cloud. He squeezed her hands. "I know you would be," he said, then chuckled. "If you were staying here."

Krystin lowered her eyes again, nodding, not really understanding him. She was trying so hard to be strong for him.

Merrick threw his head back and laughed out loud.

Krystin looked up sharply, suddenly angry at his seemingly carefree attitude about leaving. She opened her mouth to rebuke him, but stopped as Merrick grabbed her up in a tight hug.

"Oh, my sweet flower, you are going with me," he whispered in her ear.

"What? I am?" gasped Krystin barely able to breathe. "Oh, Merrick, really?"

He placed his hands on her shoulders and leaned her gently back. He lifted her chin so she could see his face as he nodded. "Yes, really. We are leaving in two days on the flagship, The Flying Shell. She's the fastest in the fleet."

The reality of a sailing voyage began to dawn on the crown matriarch, and her next words came tumbling out like water from a swift river over a steep drop.

"I've never been on a boat before. How long will it take? How long will we be there? What will I wear? What about the children? Is it safe for them on a ship? How will I manage? What about . . ."

Merrick placed his hand gently over Krystin's mouth to stop the flood of words.

"Don't worry. Mother will help you with everything. The children are staying here. It seems a little getaway will do us both some good." Merrick said grinning.

Making an astonishing recovery at the news of a sea voyage, Nizza was assigned to go along as Krystin's escort and Merrick's advisor, a fact which neither sister could stop smiling about. Merrick had reluctantly consented, telling his sister that "advisor" was merely an honorary title.

Two days later, the high patriarch, his slightly tearful wife, and very excited sister were boarding The Flying Shell amid a small crowd of palace guards and well-wishers, which included a few of the high council, Smich and Wayen, who insisted on seeing them off no-matter-what, and two uncertain toddler twins held in the arms of Leesel and Boolie.

As the grand tall-ship backed gracefully away from the docking pier and turned toward the open seas beyond the harbor, Smich and Wayen couldn't resist using their birth-gifts to give the ship a sendoff, complete with a barrage of waterblimps, a swarm of iridescent, buzzing zippers, leaping schools of aqua velvet fish along with whoops of "good luck" and "smooth sailing".

"Send us a message by catlin if you need us!" shouted Krystin to Leesel as the ship gathered speed and the seabirds called overhead. "Or a telepathic note to Merrick!"

"Mama! Dada!" cried Phyre, squirming in Leesel's clutch.

"Bye-bye" whispered Jewl, enjoying all the activity.

CHAPTER 14

The next day, Smich showed up at the palace an hour before dawn. Most would still be sleeping. He knew just how to bypass the guards stationed at each post. He ducked into the first secret passage he came to, creeping silently through the go-betweens. He had been this way many times before when he and his cousin had been out too late, or were not to go out at all.

Cracking open a secret door behind a tapestry in the upper hallway, Smich peeked out. *No one in sight. Good.* He inched down the hall toward the next door. Placing his ear on the door itself, he listened. *Nothing. Good. No one stirring yet.*

Smich carefully wrapped his fingers around the door handle, making sure it didn't rattle. He turned it firmly, but slowly, until the latch disengaged. Then he pushed it open slightly and peered in.

He waited as his eyes grew accustomed to the dimmer light. He scanned the room thoroughly. *Windows closed. Closet open. No one in the chair. Clothes strewn on the floor. Good sign. That means the servant has not been around yet either. Perfect!*

Smich slipped into the room, soundlessly closing the door behind him. His eyes settled on the figure in the bed. He wondered how he should do it. *Quietly, with my hand over the mouth? Viciously to instill fear? I must keep this quiet no matter what. I mustn't get caught this time. This is too important. Too urgent.*

Crossing the room on tip-toe, Smich approached his victim. Eagerly he stood over the unconscious lump in the bed. He smiled a small, evil smile. Gently, he eased back the covers to expose the intended's head and neck. Wanting to savor this moment a bit longer, he hesitated only for a breath. Then Smich placed his hand firmly over the sleeper's mouth. Placing his knee up on the bed, he put his other hand on the person's shoulder and began to bounce furiously up and down, while calling softly in the ear, "Irthshake! Irthshake!"

Wayen's eyes flew open as he struggled to rise, gasping for breath and trying to yell out. Smich, being the larger of the boys, held him fast, while trying desperately to control his own outburst of laughter at his cousin's distress.

Disoriented by the sudden, frightening awakening, it took Wayen several seconds to realize what had happened. Still fighting to rise and with murder in his eyes, Wayen let out a muffled "I'm going to kill you!" from his still covered mouth.

Smich released his cousin and clamped his hands over his own mouth as he doubled over, collapsing weakly on the floor. Wayen sat up, shaking his head at the disgusting display. "What is the matter with you?" he whispered angrily. "What are you doing here?"

Sucking in a breath or two to calm himself, Smich sat up on the floor and regained his composure. "You gotta come with me, Cuz. Right now! Hurry up or we'll miss the whole thing."

"What are you talking about? Miss what?" whispered Wayen as he began to pull on his clothes.

"I heard them talking. There's a meeting going on. It's starting at dawn. We gotta hurry."

"What meeting? Who?" replied Wayen.

"You, know! The X's!"

"The X's?" Wayen paused and thought. "You mean the Xens? Sweet singing shells, Smich! Are you crazy?"

"Come on, Cuz! Don't be a bumphead. This is going to be good! We can be spies for the crown!"

"We could get killed more like," replied Wayen, flopping down on the bed.

"Are you going to be a ruglump or what?" Smich's voice raised in frustration.

"Sssssshhhhh! You'll wake the palace!" hissed Wayen.

"Come on!" Smich begged, lowering his voice again. "We've talked about this lots of times. Let's do it! We'll be careful. If things get too weird, we'll leave."

"I don't know about this. These people are serious trouble, Smich."

"Well, I'm going, with or without you." Smich folded his arms across his chest and stared at his cousin. "You got ten seconds and I'm out of here. Ten . . . nine . . . eight . . . seven . . . six more seconds and you'll miss the opportunity of a lifetime . . . six . . . five . . . four . . . threeeeee . . . suffering slime slugs! Please, Wayen!

"Oh, fine! But don't cry about it when we get tied up, gagged and dumped in the sea!"

*　　*　　*

Dawn was fast approaching. Palace residents began to stir as the kitchen help began stoking the ovens in preparation for the morning meal. Servants took their time preparing themselves for their day's work. The changing of the guard happened smoothly, the night guard wearily shuffling off to their quarters to sleep.

Jewl awoke and cried, but was quickly calmed and sent back to sleep under Leesel's watchful care. The high matriarch lay awake in her bed thinking of her husband yet again, listening to the deep blue water wash up to the shore over and over and over.

Unseen by any of them, two boys had run through the palace gardens, well on their way to trouble.

CHAPTER 15

K rystin floated in her bubble just above the ship's deck. The bubble was clear and nearly form-fitting. It moved as she moved and was barely visible. She noticed now a few of the crew also had bubbles around them. She smiled to herself. *It feels better not to be the only one,* she thought as she strolled on the deck.

The crown matriarch's first morning at sea had been both exhilarating and embarrassing. She thought back to her eagerness as The Flying Shell had left its mooring, moving out into en'Edlia Bay. The brisk breeze had blown through her hair, the smell of salt water and sea life was heavy in the air. It was a glorious day, the sun created dazzling sparkles on the waves, while sea birds had called their goodbyes overhead.

The crew moved in harmony with the ship, up and down, to and fro with the captain's orders and the seas rolling waves rocking the ship back and forth, yet ever forward toward the open sea.

"Well away!" called a sailor from the upper rigging. "Smooth sailing ahead, Captain!"

"Bring her on course for Raden and hoist the sails!" Captain Acrums shouted from the upper deck at the stern.

"Aye, aye, Captain!" sang out First Mate Oyley from the main deck. "Look lively there, crew! Hoist the sails! All linens to the wind!"

Merrick had stood next to Krystin and Nizza on the main deck. They had smiled broadly at the excitement of the busy ship and the thrill of embarking on another adventure. Merrick had chattered to them about the parts of the ship and its rigging and the running of the ship in general. He was an experienced sailor. Brokt had sent him out several times as midshipman to learn the ways of the sea he loved. "If you're going to live in a realm by the sea, my son, you had better become friends with it," he quoted his father. "A good friend will serve you well."

Merrick had also been on many trade and diplomatic voyages to po'Enay, Andjardi and once to the Raden Islands with his father many years ago. Now even he was excited to return to this land of warm seas, exotic plants and sandy beaches. He called it a paradise. "If I hadn't been in line for high patriarch," Merrick had quietly told Krystin, "I might have sailed to Raden and never come back."

Nizza had gasped in outrage. "I'm telling Mother!" she cried.

Her brother laughed. "I'm sure Mother would agree with me."

As they had talked about the ship and the sea and their destination, a strange feeling had begun to come over Krystin. She had brushed it off as just being a bit nervous. This was all so new to her. The feeling of floating and all that water! Completely surrounded by it and so deep below her. It had made her feel small and helpless. She had glanced at Nizza to see if she might be feeling it too, but Nizza seemed quite happy as she leaned against the railing gazing out at the tossing sea.

Merrick had talked on excitedly. "And you'll just have to try a palm-bomb. The food on Raden to so delicious! Exotic fishes, fruits and even edible flowers. I hope King Raden doesn't demand all my time."

Krystin had felt her attention wandering as the strange feeling inside her intensified. Her head began feeling warm and her breakfast was mimicking the rolling of the waves around her. *Those waves!* she thought. *Always moving . . . rocking the ship . . . up and down . . . back and forth . . . always moving.*

Merrick had stopped talking and looked quizzically at Krystin. "Are you feeling all right?" he asked.

"Ummm . . ." Krystin replied half listening while whatever was in her stomach was threatening to reappear.

"You look absolutely green!" Nizza had cried. "Are you seasick?" Krystin didn't know what being seasick was, but she was at sea and she was feeling sick. Very sick.

Suddenly she had become violently ill as her breakfast spewed from her mouth all over the deck, splattering Merrick's boots and causing Nizza to retreat squealing.

"I guess that answers your question, Nizza," Merrick murmured. He had gently but quickly guided his wife to lean over the railing as she had continued to retch, groaning miserably in between. Nizza patted her back and used her birth-gift to comfort her.

After helping Krystin to her cabin below deck, Merrick had arranged for the ship's doctor to help her with the seasickness. The doctor's birth-gift was his ability to create a bubble which would encase a person and hold them off the ground. The encased person would feel no motion of the ship, but be able to move around either above or below deck, hence eliminating any seasickness.

"I could have chosen to work with the palace guard," Dr. Ikkin had told the couple as he checked that the bubble was complete and working properly. "I was offered a job by a very wealthy family in Leppash whose son was allergic to zippers and slappers, but when I heard of this opportunity to travel at sea, I made my decision," he stated, smiling. "No one needs to suffer on a sea voyage. At least not while I'm on duty!"

"Thank you very much, Dr. Ikkin!" Krystin had taken his hand warmly. "I think I would have died without you."

"Now remember the bubble only lasts for three days," he had cautioned. "If you feel any of your symptoms return, come see me at once."

"I will!" Krystin responded. She had waved goodbye as she and Merrick returned topside to join Nizza and truly enjoy the voyage.

*   *   *

Anxiously awaiting the arrival of The Flying Shell, King Raden Rex VIII lounged in his sandstone mansion on a huge throne of pure, priceless gold. He was a large, well-built man in the early thirty years of his life. Like everyone on the island, his skin was golden brown. His handsome features included a straight, wide nose and warm golden-brown eyes which were framed by a mass of sandy-blond curls that fell to his shoulders. An informal crown of local flowers and greenery lay off-centered on his head. He kept his golden jeweled crown in a locked chest for formal occasions, like dinner with his coming guests from en'Edlia.

Dressed in the traditional island garb of a light linen knee-length tunic, which of course had been embellished with rare gems and shells, he felt at ease. The air was warm and humid, as always. A gentle breeze from the northwest played with the sheer, white curtains at the open windows, while strings of hanging beads and shells made gentle music.

Many servants, all female, surrounded the king, tending to his every whim. He shooed away a servant who now offered him yet another cooling mawmaw drink. *Ships were so slow!* he thought. *Why didn't they just teleport down. Ha! Too bad no one has that much power. No more drinking! No more eating! Now I need time to think,* thought Raden impatiently.

"Get out! All of you!" he roared suddenly. The women jumped and stared at their king. "You heard me!" He waved his arms, rattling his shell bracelets noisily. "Get out! Prepare for our guests! Have you nothing else to do?"

His servants fled from the throne room leaving Raden alone with his thoughts. He had already heard about the daring and beautiful new crown matriarch. He was toying with ideas of how he could claim her as his own. *One more jewel in my crown, so to speak, and the crowning jewel at that.*

Raden tapped his fingertips together under his chin as he thought. *The negotiations with this young, inexperienced new high patriarch should easily go in my favor.* He well remembered Merrick as a wild and impetuous boy. Raden's father, Raden Rex VII had been king then. And he had been crown prince, carefully observing every shrewd move his father made. He thought about the high patriarch then. *Carefree and careless at times. The boy loved it here. Who doesn't?* he thought, smiling broadly.

"I, King Raden Rex VIII, will keep him happy and entertained on my island paradise. It will all be so easy." He spoke out loud now. "I have so many lovely maidens here to charm and woo him while we negotiate new terms of trade. Not to mention my secret weapon!" He rubbed his huge hands together and grinned.

"I will agree to trade on my terms! He will have to give much to meet my demands." The king leaned forward in anticipation. "Perhaps more than he knows!"

Raden laughed out loud then clapped his hands together. His cautious servants peered into the room nervously. "Where have you been?" cried the king happily. "Come! Bring me refreshments! Play some fine music! Dance for me! Sing a happy song! We have guests coming! It is to be a wonderful time!"

The king clapped his hands in time with the music. He grinned as he thought of the prize he was sure to win for himself.

CHAPTER 16

The meeting had already begun as Smich and Wayen inched their way closer to the dim, smoky room's open window in the back of a ramshackle building. There weren't many who actually lived in the poor sector of the city, at least compared to the whole city itself. The high patriarchs of the past had never liked that this place even existed. They had tried very hard to make improvements, pass laws and provide funds to bring this sector back to a healthy state. It was as if it kept fighting back, not wanting a cure or a healing. It seemed to cling to the festering social sicknesses which bred within it like an addiction.

The poor sector, commonly called The Shards, was a place you avoided, if you had any sense at all. Nothing good ever happened here, unless it was a death. That would be a blessed end to a miserable existence for sure.

Yet Smich seemed magnetized to The Shards like an Irth Star to the night sky. It gave him a heightened sense of being alive. It felt dangerous, keeping him on edge. He loved it. His own life seemed dull, even boring, and much the same every day. Here in The Shards, everything was an adventure with certain death hovering at your shoulder. Smich's only problem was he couldn't go alone. Company always made him feel braver.

"I can't believe I let you drag me here!" Wayen whispered fiercely.

"Shut up and listen!" Smich hissed back.

The place was called The Shards because the people who came to live here were like the shards, or small broken pieces of shells which were pushed up on the beach by the tides. Cast-offs of the sea, they were shunned by all as sharp, hurting things to avoid, having no value or beauty. The people here felt bruised, they were hurting for some reason, not always physically. Some had been cast off by their own family. Some came here like Smich, drawn by fascination only to get involved with something tragic or illegal for which no other place would have them. Some were workers of dark magic by choice, thinking their ways were better, more pure somehow. Some were just sad, poor, lost or down on their luck. It didn't matter the reason. The Shards took them all in, never letting them leave. There had been a few escape artists who managed by some miracle to fight and claw their way out, but it was very few indeed.

Sometimes the shell shards were collected from the beaches, ground to powder and mixed with the soil to improve the mineral content. There were only two times any of those who lived in The Shards were collected—when going to prison or when it was time to be put permanently and mercifully below the soil.

"The crown matriarch must die!" A harsh voice reached the straining ears of two eavesdropping boys concealed in the grimy shadows of early morning.

"And those two brats of hers as well!"

"Magicless half breeds!"

"M.O.W.s!"

"What's a M.O.W.?" whispered Wayen as more insulting, angry words erupted from around the room.

"You are so sheltered!" Smich hissed. "The letters stand for Magicless Off-Worlder. Now keep quiet!"

The boys crouched below the open window of the meeting room. They raised themselves up slightly to get a peek inside at the Xens.

It was a small, unkempt room with many grungy people sitting on mismatched chairs or standing around facing the far left side of the room where a small table sat. A giant-of-a-man sat slouched on a wooden barrel behind that table. His unshaven face wore a terrible scowl. His sparse, storm-cloud gray hair rained down his forehead which was lined and deeply tanned. Heavy black eyebrows crashed together over his piercing pale-blue eyes. His shabby clothes were much like the rest in the room.

"There are women in there too," Wayen muttered, surprised by the mix of people. He had been expecting a few evil men, but most of these people just looked sad and poor. He made a face at the smell of unwashed bodies, wood smoke, alcohol, and pungent incense burning somewhere, trying unsuccessfully to cover all the other wretched odors. It stung his eyes and tickled his nose. He rubbed it vigorously to stop from sneezing.

Smich rolled his eyes, putting his finger to his lips. Sometimes his cousin could be so exasperating! He turned his attention back to the meeting's discussion, straining to hear every word.

"So what are we going to do about it?" The giant man stood up behind the wobbly table at the far end of the room. "All I hear is talk!" He slammed his fist down, splintering the table top and nearly collapsing it. The room went deadly silent, and he continued in a low voice.

"We all know the obvious. The high patriarch has betrayed us as did his father. His kind cares nothing for the purity of our race or of our world. He has brought in a weakness, a disease which will infect us all! Why does he not see it? Because he has been bewitched! Entranced by this off-worlder! Who knows what power she wields secretly?"

There was a murmur of agreement around the room. A woman's voice spoke, addressing the giant speaker, "Bocja, I heard she herself killed the great Zarcon!"

Another man said, "She talks to dragons for sure! Perhaps she controls Merrick like she did that dragon." Another murmur, filled with fear, circled the room.

"We must do away with her!" one cried out fearfully.

"She must be in league with our enemies!"

"Enough!" Bocja yelled, silencing them again. "Rumors are for old, silly am'Orans! You are all worthless breakfast bugs! You buzz around just waiting to be inhaled by the ruling system. And then what? You are dead! Or worse! Spit out to suffer unnoticed, unheeded. None of you have any idea what to do but waggle your tongues. But I know what we must do!"

Bocja lowered his voice to nearly a whisper. "I have a plan."

The room erupted with questions.

Outside Wayen looked wide-eyed at Smich, jerking his head to the side indicating his desire to get out of there now. Smich lowered his eyebrows in a deep frown, shaking his head. Wayen pointed away. Smich folded his arms. Wayen began to get up from his crouched position, but Smich grabbed him roughly, pulling him back down.

"This is just getting good!" Smich whispered fiercely. "We can't go now."

"Now is the best time to go," Wayen threw back at him. "Before we hear any more! The less we know the better."

"We just got to find out what the plan is, don't you see?"

"No, I do not! People have been killed for less."

"You're such a ruglump."

"And you're crazy."

The loud voice of Bocja stopped their argument. Both boys jumped and crouched lower, ducking under some broken crates piled up against the building.

"I tell you I have already put it into motion! I have a man on board The Flying Shell. He has his instructions. He knows what to do. Any chance he gets to get rid of her, he will, make no mistake."

"And what if that doesn't work?" angrily questioned a young man.

"Then the second part of my plan will come into play. I have a guarantee it is foolproof."

"How can you be so sure?" the young man challenged Bocja again.

"Look, you," Bocja spoke. "I know what you want, but I'm not doing this for revenge. This is for the good of all Irth. Don't you get it?"

Embarrassed, the young man stormed out of the room, turning right towards Smich and Wayen. Using his birth-gift, Smich caused a bottle to roll down the other side of the street drawing the man's attention away. Caught up in his own anger, he marched past the boys without even a glance.

Wayen's face was white and sweaty when Smich looked back at him. He dared not show his cousin his own fear, so he smiled grimly and shrugged.

As Smich edged back toward the window, Bocja was eyeing those in the room critically. "Well, anybody else got anything to say?" he demanded. There were low mumblings and shaking of heads, but no one spoke up. "Good. Then we stick to my plan. Keep your ears open. Meet me here same time next week and be ready to report what you've heard."

Wayen made a move to go, but Smich grabbed him, shaking his head adamantly pointing to the open window. Wayen couldn't stand it any longer. He gave his cousin a fierce look and called a small swarm of slappers into the meeting room to keep the Xens' attention occupied, while Smich, picking up on Wayen's lead, toppled over the broken table in the meeting room.

Well, there goes that table," a woman snickered.

"Blasted slappers!" hissed Bocja, moving away from the window. "Where'd they come from?"

The boys made a quick and quiet getaway from The Shards. They were seen by a few, who just shook their heads and guffawed at two frightened-looking boys racing down the street like they were being chased by a hoard of demons.

Back at the meeting room, Bocja sat thinking about his plan. This deal had cost him plenty. *It had better work or someone would pay, and pay dearly,* he thought as he flipped his knife in the air.

CHAPTER 17

The Flying Shell moved through the waters of en'Edlia Bay with skilled precision. Captain Acrums knew his ship well and just how to handle her. He knew his crew too. Most had been with him for years. However, he had to hire on three new sailors for this voyage as some were due a shore leave in en'Edlia. So he had signed on some who seemed skilled enough and had experience on dangerous straits and the open seas.

Now he watched them with care, pointing them out to First Mate Oyley to watch over as well. Acrums would have no ruglumps on this trip. He took his duty seriously as flag ship commander, second only to High Mariner Cebton, Commander of the Sea Forces of en'Edlia. It was his great honor to safely escort the high patriarch and his company on this important diplomatic mission to the Raden Islands and back.

They sailed out of en'Edlia Bay, past Snail Island and into the am'Oran Sea. Passing between am'Oran Island and Spider Island, they sailed near the coast of po'Enay. Krystin wished they could stop for a tour of po'Enay City, but Merrick had to promise that trip for another time.

Skirting around Sea Plum Island on the third day out at sea, finally past the last of the am'Oran Islands, the captain began to relax. No storms on the horizon. He had tried to hire on a weatherer for the trip—one with the birth-gift to move or change the weather—but no one was available. His own crew's weatherer, Talia, was taking her shore leave and refused to pull extra duty even at the offer of increased pay. "Been away from my family too long already!" she claimed. Acrums shook his head. Couldn't blame the sailor for that.

Thus far there had been no trouble with the new crew. He glanced over at Manx who was hauling away at the rigging ropes, letting out extra sails to catch the prevailing winds. Teeto was amidships swabbing the main deck and Avidd was busy at the stern. They seemed to know what they were doing, following orders without question.

There were no problems with the patriarchal party, aside from a bout of seasickness which was easily handled. He looked with fondness on the young couple as they leaned against the railing on the port bow, happily talking and watching the horizon. The captain remembered when he was young and in love. He sighed as he patted his now mature figure and thought of his lonely wife at home.

This will be a good voyage, thought the captain. Once they rounded the Razor's Jaw, they would make good time on the open waters of the ed'Yrran Sea. The Razor's Jaw was a wicked point of land which jutted out separating the am'Oran and ed'Yrran Seas. It kept the am'Oran Sea somewhat sheltered from the harsher weather of the open sea, but was also the cause of many a shipwreck in a storm. Captain Acrums always gave it a wide berth.

It was another day and a half southwest to the islands. Beyond the islands, another day's journey south, lay Andjardi. Acrums smiled and shook his head. He had sailed to Andjardi many times and loved the food there. Spicy and rich, greasy and hot. His mouth watered at the thought. *Ah, well,* he thought. *The islands have their pleasures too.* He and the crew would take a few days of shore leave during the trade negotiations. *Yes, it was going to be a good voyage indeed.*

*   *   *

"Manx! Get on those ropes!" Oyley yelled above the howling wind. "Avidd! Get those sails secured!" The storm had surprised them in the very early hours of the morning of the fourth day, sweeping up from the ed'Yrran Sea to the south. The night crew was still on duty when the alarm was sounded. The whole crew reported for duty before the sun was up.

Merrick lost his footing on the rain-soaked deck and nearly went sprawling. He left Krystin and Nizza in their cabins, coming topside to see if he could help the crew. Clinging to a railing, he steadied himself as he approached the captain. "Begging the captain's pardon, but might I be of assistance?" he respectfully addressed Acrums at the top of his lungs.

The captain's eyes were focused on the rapidly advancing black clouds and crackling lightning in the dim light. The crew raced over the ship like ants, booming thunder beating echoes in their chests. As the heightened swells crashed over the decks, they quickly tied themselves to safety lines to keep from being swept overboard. Wind violently whipped at the remaining sail which had not been stowed, threatening to tear it to shreds.

"The rigging seems to be jammed aloft somewhere!" shouted Acrums back at the patriarch. "Can you manage it?"

Merrick gave a quick nod, went sliding down the steps, and onto the main deck at a run. He peered up at the mast, squinting into the rain, trying to see what the problem was. Then he saw it. One of the ropes had doubled up in the pulley, being soaked and swollen from the storm.

"You there!" he yelled to Teeto. "Come aloft with me!"

"Aye, sir!"

They sprang onto the rigging, climbing unsteadily. The wind, gusting to gale force, tried to rip them from the ropes and fling them into the frothing sea. The rain beat upon them, blurring their vision, making each handhold slippery at best. Yet still they climbed.

"There!" Merrick shouted to the sailor with him. "See the pulley!"

Teeto nodded. He maneuvered closer, in the spider web of ropes. Reaching out, he stretched to grab the knotted mass.

Merrick glanced down as the ship leaned dangerously over on its port side. The waves suddenly seemed as if they were going to swallow him as he gripped the ropes with all his might.

The ship lurched back upright, the mast acting like a whip. Teeto suddenly lost his grip and tumbled from the rigging toward the rocking deck far below. His scream rose above the storm.

"CAPTAIN! MAN DOWN!" Merrick shouted while simultaneously sending a thought to Acrums.

Captain Acrums' head jerked up. His sharp eyes caught sight of the crewman plummeting toward the deck. He spoke a word, unheard in the gale, invoking his birth-gift into action.

Merrick held his breath as he clung to the swinging rigging, waiting for the sickening thud of the man's impact on the hard, wooden decking. The seconds ticked away in his mind, but that sound never came.

Had the sailor fallen into the sea with the rolling of the ship? Merrick wondered. He chanced a look down. There, mere inches off the forward deck, Teeto floated spread-eagle, his scream having died to a moan. The captain made a downward movement with his hand controlling the sailor as he gently brought him to rest on the deck, as a wave soaked Teeto with seawater. He jumped up, unharmed, and secured himself to a safety line.

Merrick shook his head in wonder. It was a good birth-gift for a ship's captain he supposed. *The safety of his crew is the captain's most important concern.*

Now the knotted rope was Merrick's concern. His birth-gift would not help him here. He steadied his grip, shook the hair off his face, and moved toward the pulley, inching his way closer as the ship continued to buck and roll wildly in the worsening storm.

Watching from the aft deck below, Manx saw the high patriarch would be out of the way for some time. Everyone else was busy above board. *Everyone but the crown matriarch and her little helper*, he thought. Manx edged around the railing, playing out his safety line. He ducked under some rigging. Untying his line, he shouldered a coil of rope and stole to the hatch unnoticed. As he opened the companionway doors, he was washed down the steps and into the cabins' hallway with the next crashing wave.

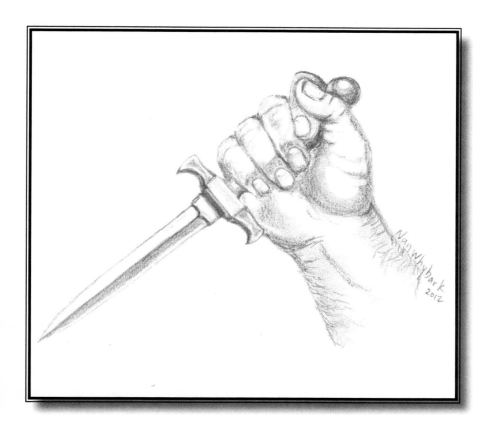

CHAPTER 18

Krystin stood in her tiny cabin, bracing herself with her outstretched arms, clinging to the built-in furniture on either side. She was battling her panic in the heaving ship around her. She was grateful she could not feel the true motion of it in her new bubble.

As he had predicted, Dr. Ikkin's first bubble had begun to deteriorate by the end of the third day at sea. Feeling woozy, she had found her way to his room again. He had formed a new one for her, thankfully before the storm had come upon them.

At the storm's onset, Captain Acrums had immediately confined her and Nizza to their quarters. Even though Krystin had her bubble, it wouldn't keep her from being tossed overboard by the winds and waves. It didn't keep her from being frightened by the bucking and rocking of the ship.

Nizza, who had come to her sister's cabin for her own comfort as well as Krystin's, was now wishing she had a bubble too. Nizza lay in the bunk feeling quite ill. She had been fine with the gentle motion of the ship on fair seas, but this was more than she could handle. Dr. Ikkin had been too busy to make a bubble for her. He had told her she would just have to wait it out.

Not only was she green with nausea, Nizza was more scared than she had ever been in her life. She clung to the bunk railing not knowing whether to throw up or scream. She clenched her teeth, trying not to cry. It seemed to her the sloshing water on the floor could quickly deepen at any moment to drown her. She pictured the green, salty water getting deeper and deeper then bursting through the cabin door. She imagined herself surrounded by water, holding her breath, swimming up and up, her lungs crying out for air.

Seeing Krystin's panicky face, Nizza knew she would just make things worse if she didn't try to keep calm. She tried to focus on her blanket's fuzzy feeling as she felt the bile rising in her throat.

Krystin glanced down at Nizza's off-colored face and was filled with concern. She wished Merrick would come back. His presence would give both of them comfort. She wished he wasn't so willing to put himself in harm's way. He was brave, but seemed reckless at times. She certainly didn't want to lose him now!

There was a gentle knock on the cabin door. *There he is now,* Krystin sighed with relief. She steadied herself and moved to open the door.

"Oh!" cried Krystin, taking a step back as she came face to face with one of the crew, drenched, dripping, and stinking of seawater. "I thought you were my husband." She blushed, feeling foolish.

"Begging yer pardon, Crown Matriarch, but I've come on yer husband's bidding," the sailor began, mopping his face with a rag. "I've brought ye a message."

Krystin relaxed. "Oh, thank you, ah . . . ah . . ."

"Name's Manx, Highness," he said while fumbling in his inner vest pocket. "Sorry, it might be a bit wet."

"Yes, of course. The storm." Krystin edged closer to him, one hand anxiously reaching for the expected note, the other clinging to any handhold she could find.

Manx stepped into the cabin as he pretended to hunt for the note. With the ship's next lurch, he launched himself forward, crashing into Krystin. He grabbed her wrist with one hand, twisting it painfully as he back kicked the cabin door shut.

"Ow! You're hurting me!" she cried out. "Let go!" She stumbled backward under the man's advancing weight, getting the breath knocked out of her as they forcefully hit the wall together.

"What are you doing?" Nizza gasped and tried to struggle out of the bunk to help her sister. She was weak and the effort made her head spin. Still she tried to push herself up.

Manx kept a tight grip on the crown matriarch, pinning her up against the wall. With his other hand he slid out the dagger he had concealed, and brought it to her throat.

"There now, missy," Manx whispered between his teeth.

The color drained from Krystin's face as she felt the blade in his hand. "What are you doing?" she gasped, frozen with fear.

"Just delivering a message, like I said, missy. Or should I say WITCH!" he hissed in her face.

Krystin jerked her head away from his foul breath and spittle on her cheek. "What are you talking about?" She struggled to keep her voice from shaking. She had to keep him talking. "I'm not a witch. I have no magical powers."

"So ye say! Silence now! Ye're not casting any evil spells on me!" Manx released her wrist, and quickly moved his hand up to cover her mouth, but not before she let out a scream.

Nizza cried out as well, still struggling with the blankets which had wrapped around her legs.

Manx's eyes squinted with anger. "Stay in the bunk, brat!" he growled at Nizza, pressing the blade harder against Krystin's throat. "Ye moves and the witch here gets it!" Then he smiled wickedly as he saw tears well up in his victim's eyes. "Not that anyone will hear ye over the storm." He laughed then. "And of course me birth-gift! I can absorb all sound around me. So scream all y'like! There'll be no one hearing anything!"

At that moment the ship was thrown over on its side, off-balancing Manx so that he stumbled back, momentarily freeing his intended victim.

"HELP! SOMEONE HELP ME!" Krystin screamed. She tried to throw herself past her attacker to reach the door, but he was quickly on his feet, cutting off her escape. She screamed and thrashed her arms so he couldn't get hold of her again.

Krystin felt a sting and cried out. She froze at the sight of her own blood dripping from a fresh cut on her arm. She immediately pulled down her sleeve to cover it, applying pressure with her other hand to stop the bleeding. Now she was cornered again.

"Here's the message!" Manx snarled as he grabbed her roughly, forcing her back against the wall, his blade pricking her cheek painfully. "Yer princey don't love you no more!"

"That's not true!" Krystin sobbed.

"Nobody in en'Edlia loves ye no more!" he continued viciously. "Nobody wants ye around no more, so I've come to make sure ye don't come back! EVER!"

"No! NO!" cried Krystin as Manx snickered wickedly in her face.

"Let her go!" cried Nizza. Her head was spinning. She felt nauseated as she sat up.

"I warned ye, brat!" yelled Manx, as he tried to backhand her. Jerking back she made an effort to kick out at Manx. Her kick was weak. She was off-balanced, banging her head painfully on the bunk. Everything went black as she fell back onto the pillow. Yet she could hear the sailor continue to talk as she struggled to remain conscious.

"Got any last words? I got a good memory so's I won't forget nothing." He smiled broadly showing a mouthful of yellowed, rotting teeth.

"Yes, I do have something to say," Krystin whispered, trying desperately to keep calm and think. "But . . . you'll have to lean closer. I'm . . . I'm too frightened to talk louder."

"As well ye should be, missy," Manx replied meanly, leaning in, putting his ear near her lips. "Get ready to die like the witch ye are."

Krystal began to whisper, "Please, tell Merrick I love him, and remember that . . ." then suddenly she bit his ear as hard as she could and hung on. Manx screamed at the unexpected attack.

Krystin brought her hand up between his knife hand and her throat. Shoving it away, she rammed his hand against the end of the bunk. Manx dropped the knife, yowling as he tried to pull away from Krystin's painful biting.

Then she grabbed onto his shirt with one hand. With her other, she grabbed and pulled on his other ear, digging her nails into his flesh. Manx howled in pain and tried to pry her hands away.

Next she kicked his shins and stomped on the tops of his feet, all the while he cursed and flailed, trying to protect himself from his victim turned attacker. He finally ripped his ear from her mouth, while Krystin tried not to gag at the salty, dirty-flesh taste in her mouth.

Manx bent to recover his blade, but then Krystin landed a powerful kick to his knee. There was a loud *pop!* Manx cursed as his leg gave way. Krystin shoved him to one side as he collapsed. She rushed out of his reach, as Nizza, her head spinning, tried again to rise from the bunk to help.

Cursing and squirming to fetch his weapon, Manx floundered on the floor as the seawater sloshed around him. Nizza finally flailed her way out of the bed just in time to throw up all over Manx.

All at once, the cabin door opened, and the doctor stood there staring. Seeing the situation, he advanced on Manx, grabbed him by the back of the shirt and threw him against the built-in cabinets. Manx turned to fight, so Ikkin rammed Manx headfirst into the bunks. The sailor crumpled in an unconscious heap on the floor.

"Oh, Doctor!" Krystin cried, nearly collapsing on the floor herself. The doctor moved quickly to take her arm.

"I remembered the young miss wanted a bubble, so I came to see how you were getting along," remarked the doctor. "It looks like it's a good thing I did."

"Thank you! I don't think I could have held him off much longer."

"Between the two of you, it looks like this man took quite a beating," the doctor remarked as he lifted the unconscious sailor out of the sloshing seawater. "Please go to my healing room and wait while I have him locked up."

Ikkin called Oyley from the deck and he, along with two others hauled Manx off, locking him in the brig. Then the doctor returned to his healing room to properly dress Krystin's wound and see to Nizza's illness as well as the large lump on her head.

Merrick was also summoned and was instantly at his wife's side. Anxious feelings of concern, anger and relief washed over him as she related the story of how Manx had come to kill her. "I'll not leave you alone again," Merrick vowed. He escorted her back to their cabin after seeing that Nizza, also badly shaken, locked herself in her own cabin to wait out the storm in her new bubble.

"No doubt the Xens were behind this attack," Merrick said mostly to himself once he had his wife settled in the bunk. "I'll have to be more attentive. The enemy is everywhere. I have fooled myself to think less of the situation." He gently squeezed Krystin's hand as she drifted off in an exhausted sleep, the ship still pitching in the dying storm.

* * *

The morning broke clear and calm for the Flying Shell on the ed'Yrran Sea, unlike Manx in the brig.

"Get her away from me!" he shrieked, his eyes wide in the fossi-shell's light. "She's a wild witch, she is! Was going to eat me alive! Bit me ear off, she did!" He had backed away as far as he could in his tiny prison cell in the dark, dank ship's hold. "Keep her away from me!" he yelled pointing at Krystin.

The captain had asked Krystin to identify her attacker so charges could be made and sentence pronounced. He had heard her testimony plus that of Nizza and Dr. Ikkin earlier. Now the crown matriarch and her husband stood before an extremely nervous Manx with the captain and first mate Oyley.

"Is this the man who attacked you?" Captain Acrums directed the question at Krystin.

"Don't let her get me," whimpered Manx, hunkering down in a corner.

"Yes, Captain, that's the man," she replied.

"Do you deny you attacked this woman with intent to kill her?" Acrums demanded of the prisoner.

"No, I mean yes . . . . I mean . . . just keep her away, Cap'in. Please . . . I'll do anything," Manx cried.

"Just answer the question, ye bottom spider!" barked the Captain.

"Yes, I meant to kill her!" Manx yelled crazily. "She's a witch! She's going to ruin the whole world!"

"Who put you up to this?"

"No M.O.W.s! No M.O.W.S!" he began to chant.

"Silence!" Acrums ordered, then grinned. "Or I'll let our crown matriarch do what she will with you!"

Manx threw himself on the brig floor. "Not that! No, Cap'in!"

"Then tell me who is behind this attempt at murder."

"The Xens, like I said, Cap'in," blubbered Manx. "They made me do it."

"And who's the leader of the Xens?" asked Merrick.

"Don't make me say, Cap'in," pleaded the prisoner. "They'll kill me if I tell."

"The high patriarch can just look in your head and find the name. It's his birth-gift," offered the captain. "But you'll hang for treason and for your violence against the crown matriarch."

"If you offer the information, Manx, we may be more lenient with you," stated Merrick.

"If I give it or he takes it, I'm dead either way," muttered the convicted man.

"Oh, there is one more way," the captain said slyly, motioning Krystin forward.

"Oyley!" said Acrums to his first mate. "Give me the key."

"No, Cap'in! Nooooooo!" The prisoner scrambled backward. "Don't let her have me!" Manx had such a look of terror in his wide eyes that Krystin nearly felt sorry for him. The captain looked at Krystin, giving her a wink unseen by Manx.

"Well, he's probably right. Best wait till we get to the island so you can make a proper feast of him," he said. "We'll keep him alive till then. Fresh meat is always better."

Krystin smiled and licked her dry lips. That had just the right effect on the convicted man.

"Aaah!" he screamed. "All right! I'll tell! Just promise ye won't let her eat me! Promise, Cap'in! I'll believe if ye give yer seaman's oath!"

"Then out with it, Manx! Name the leader!" shouted Merrick.

Manx cringed in his cage. The struggle in his mind was clear in his countenance. Death was staring him in the face, he just had to choose how to meet it.

"Manx!" Acrums yelled.

"Swear by the oath!" the condemned sailor seethed.

"Very well, I swear," stated Acrums.

"What about him?" Manx said pointing to Merrick.

"I am bound by Captain Acrums oath as he is captain of this ship," Merrick replied. "Now name the leader of the Xens!"

The prisoner's eyed flickered nervously between the captain, Merrick and Krystin. "It's . . . it's . . ." he gripped the cell bars. "It's . . . Bocja. In The Shards." He covered his head with his hands. "There now! I'm a dead man!" the prisoner curled up, his head on his knees. "I'm dead for sure." His voice was low and somber. "I'm a shard fit for grinding."

"Keep a watch on him, Oyley," ordered the captain, and then turned to Krystin. "Thank you, Crown Matriarch, you may return to your cabin."

"I'd like to head up to the deck for some fresh air, with your permission," Krystin stated.

"As you wish, Matriarch," the Captain replied. "High Patriarch," he bowed.

Krystin turned away, glad to be done with that ordeal. She heard Manx shout out as she took the stairs up to the deck, "You'll not have me now, witch! I'd rather die at the hands of a friend than the likes of ye!"

As she and Merrick stood on the main deck, Krystin found she was shaking. Merrick slipped his cloak around her, but it did little to calm her. She tried to clear her mind to relax herself. She was unsure if she was shaking with fear or outrage. This was more than she had expected when she came to en'Edlia. Her world had been suspicious of Merrick at first, but then had welcomed him. But this world . . . *Will I ever be fully welcome here?* she wondered.

"The moment the weather clears," Merrick stated, "I am sending a catlin to Degler ordering him to arrest this Bocja and hold him in prison. He will face trial when we return to en'Edlia. I'll have him round up anyone else even remotely connected with this man." Merrick looked into his wife's pale face. "We will disband these Xens once and for all, I swear it!"

Feeling like the whole crew was watching, she was uncertain who was an enemy or who was a friend anymore. Still shaken from her brush with death, she stayed close to Merrick for the rest of the voyage.

She confessed to Merrick she would be glad when the trip was over and they were on land again. He smiled and said, "Then you will be glad to hear we will be in the City of the Kings by tomorrow at sunset."

"Good!" Krystin retorted. "Then maybe I can rest. I'm not sure how much more adventure I can take for one trip."

Merrick laughed then. "You'll see! The islands are a paradise!

CHAPTER 19

"That's not true!" protested Wayen. "It was Smich's idea!"

The boys cowered before the oracle, Ardloh, who was in a foul mood at discovering the boys had been to a meeting of the Xens in the Shards. They all stood in Wayen's room, where the oracle had demanded they meet.

"That is entirely beside the point!" Ardloh thundered. "What did you hope to gain from such a venture?"

"Going to the Shards was more exciting than hanging around the palace all morning," Smich said honestly. "We weren't even seen."

"Oh, you were seen all right," retorted Ardloh. "Seen and identified! Not only by our spies in the Shard, but also by those of, shall we say, lesser ideals." He smiled harshly.

"So what?" countered Smich. "What are they going to do? We might never go back there again."

"And you would be wise not to," advised the oracle. "We are not the only ones with spies. They will have assassins about as well."

Wayen gulped. "But why would they want to kill us. We're just a couple of kids!"

Ardloh placed his hand on Wayen's shoulder and said, "You overheard some plans, did you not?"

"How did you know that?" asked Wayen.

"I'm not called the oracle for nothing," the man replied, a grin touching his lips briefly. "I know all about your little adventure and the ripples it has caused throughout en'Edlia."

"Ripples?" Smich piped in. "What do you mean?"

"Like a tiny pebble tossed into a pond, the ripples extend to the water's very edge."

"What?" Smich said, confused.

"I mean meddling in things which don't concern you has caused some serious problems for the high patriarchal family, and that includes both of you."

"Oh," replied Smich, hanging his head.

"What kind of problems, Ardloh?" asked Wayen.

"As you know," the oracle began, "the Xens do not approve of Merrick's choice to marry an off-worlder which will introduce the possibility of an heir to the Patriarchal Order having no birth-gift. The Xens feel this will pollute the ruling line and result in weakness in our leadership. They are plotting a way to either dethrone the high patriarch or murder the crown matriarch before she has a son. Their daughters are already a threat as they could enter a leadership position if no son is born."

"But what does that have to do with us?" Smich cried.

"You have seen the faces of those involved in this plan of treason. You have heard their plans. That makes you an assassin's target as well."

"Us?" squeaked Wayen. "We're going to get killed! I told you!" he yelled at his cousin.

"Don't be such a breakfast bug, Wayen!" Smich growled.

"Wayen is right to be frightened, young Smich," scolded the oracle. "You should have more respect for those who wield the dark magics. There has already been an attempt on the life of the crown matriarch since they've been gone."

Wayen's face turned white and his hand shook as he placed it on the sleeve of the oracle. "Is she . . . is she all right, Ardloh?"

"Yes, young master, she is just fine. Krystin is proving herself quite a fighter, in more ways than one."

Smich was still worried about his own fate. "So what's going to happen with us? Do we have to be confined to our rooms or placed under guard for the rest of our lives?"

"Yes, Ardloh, what shall we do?" Wayen asked anxiously.

Ardloh's face grew deadly serious. He glanced back and forth between the two boys with his arms folded across his chest. "You have been sentenced to house arrest under the watchful eyes of your mothers. Each to your own dwelling."

A look of horror filled their faces as they realized the depth of their punishment.

"But . . . ." they cried at once.

"I have other business to attend to," stated the oracle. "Smich you will come with me now." He gripped Smich's arm and before either of the boys could say another word in protest, he and Smich vanished from the palace. "And stay out of trouble!" his voice came to Wayen out of the air.

*   *   *

One of the crew brought Manx his meager supper. The prisoner spoke quietly to his former mate as he slid the food tray under the brig's heavy iron-barred door.

Suddenly Manx grabbed the startled man and slammed him against the bars with such force the other sailor collapsed, dazed. With desperation in his glazed eyes, Manx grabbed the keys from his mate's belt and stole out of the cell, locking the other inside.

In the dark corridors of the ship's hold, no one even noticed the once-captive man limping topside, making his way aft.

All at once, someone cried out, "The prisoner's escaped! Search the ship!" The sailors became more alert and on guard. They moved steadily over the ship like hungry skitters on the trail of the last scrap of muffybread.

"There he is!" a sailor called out. "It's Manx, there astern!"

Manx hobbled for the railing, as the crew closed in on him. They had been his mates, but there was no tolerance for treason among them.

"Come quietly now, Manx," Teeto said gently. "And ye'll get a fair trial in en'Edlia."

In the blue light of their fossi-shells, they could see the whites of the convicted man's crazed eyes. He clung to the railing shaking his head, muttering. "No . . . no . . . she'll not have me! I'll not let ye give me up to the witch!"

"Come now, there's no witch." They tried to pacify his fears as they closed ranks on him. "You'll be safe with us."

Oyley stepped forward quickly, catching Manx by the arm. "Back to the brig with ye, and no more tricks!"

Manx screamed at his touch, twisting away. He glanced once at the crew then jumped over the railing, vanishing into the black night and the foaming waves of the ship's wake.

The crew rushed to the edge to try to catch a glimpse of the desperate man and throw him a rope. Though they stood at the rail several minutes watching for a head to bob to the surface, Manx was never seen again.

CHAPTER 20

"Welcome to the City of the Kings!" King Raden Rex VIII stood on the end of the pier with open arms. A moment before he had been in his own private quarters admiring himself in his wall of mirrors. His birth-gift was self-teleportation. He could just pop in anytime, anywhere within twenty miles. It was very convenient for him when traveling around his island kingdom. The people knew him as the father figure of their nation, but having even your father just pop in on you without warning can be unnerving.

The king could also take anyone with him who was touching his person. That fact tended to make his subjects a bit edgy in his presence. Plus there was the fact he had the power to condemn anyone to death with just a word. Needless to say, most of the islanders were very good citizens, or at least pretended to be most of the time.

The king was dressed in his finest white linen tunic. It was embroidered with precious gold and purple threads in an intricate pattern which was intertwined with precious gems and colorful shells at the hem, neck, and ends of the three-quarter length sleeves. He had a fresh, green wreath on his head to denote his royalty. His bronze hands were sparkling with gold rings and bracelets.

The king wore the emblem of his small island kingdom around his neck on a heavy gold chain. The Wind Kahn, a seabird with its wings in a "V" shape as if in flight, stood for grace, beauty, serenity, and independence. Its red-tipped white wings and tail were made from tiny bits of inlaid shells and jewels; its body of a single shell carved to look like a feathered breast; its long beak and legs of finest gold; its eyes, a matched pair of glittering aquamarine gems. It was resplendent in the evening sun.

The Flying Shell eased into the harbor, gliding to the pier as the sun began its glorious descent below the horizon in a fiery blaze of red, purple, gold and pink. The crew tied off the ship and lowered the gangplank to permit the high patriarch and his party safe passage onto the pier.

So now King Raden, after arranging suitable transport for his guests, had just popped out to the ship's landing pier. One of the sailors was so surprised he fell off the dock and had to be levitated out of the water. Of course this didn't bother Raden in the least. He felt no apology was needed for his presence and its consequences, expected or not.

After a fierce hug, which left Merrick gasping for breath, and a quick glance up and down the nervous Nizza, King Raden had turned his hungry eyes upon the now blushing crown matriarch.

"High Patriarch!" Raden bellowed. "You have a new treasure in en'Edlia! Keeping secrets are you?" The king gently kissed Krystin's hand, which she withdrew too quickly, her cheeks blazing like the sunset at Raden's rapt attention.

"It has been no secret, Your Highness," Merrick replied, smiling as he put his arm around his wife. "You were invited to en'Edlia for all the ceremonies when we arrived."

"Ah, yes," the king waved off the comment. "You know I'm not much for foreign formalities. Besides," he went on quickly, "I had pressing business of my own."

"So now we come to you," Merrick bowed slightly, "as representatives of en'Edlia's Realm and High Council as trade diplomats."

Raden accepted the bow with a nod as his eyes moved back to Krystin. "This one represents en'Edlia's beauty well," he said with a grin.

"She has caused quite a stir in en'Edlia," Merrick replied. Krystin frowned at his comment, understanding all too well what he meant.

"We shall esteem her well above treasure here in my humble kingdom as well, High Patriarch." Again Raden's eyes took in the crown matriarch as he bowed before her. "But come! I am being a negligent host! Come to the Manor House near my estate to rest and eat. Refresh yourselves after your long voyage."

Raden Rex called his servants to come forward to collect the visiting group's baggage, chests and trunks as he led them toward the waiting transport. "This is Cemers'ed," he introduced one of the women to Krystin. "She will be your personal servant while you are my guest here." Krystin nodded graciously to the king, then smiled warmly at Cemers'ed as the young woman bent to quickly pick up some of the baggage.

Krystin tightened her grip on Merrick's arm as she saw they would be riding in a small but elegant wheeled-cart pulled by two huge, gold, black and cream-colored cats. The animals were twice the size of forest cats which lived in the mountains around Lyndell, and they stood nearly the same height as she. Their speckled coats were sleek, shining in the fading sunlight. Turning their large bright-green eyes upon the approaching party, they growled gently, showing white, dagger-sized teeth.

Leaving Krystin at a distance, Merrick approached the cats confidently, giving each a good scratch under the chin. Their growls turned to deep purring, pink tongues lolling out as they panted in the heat. "I see you still breed the big cats, King Raden," he remarked.

"Of course," replied the king. "The spectars are animals fit for a king. They demand respect, as do I. Not like those ridiculous hordles you raise in en'Edlia." He laughed.

"Naturally," Merrick replied, taking the insult in stride. "We all deserve respect, do we not?"

"Bah!" the king scoffed. "Respect is not to be expected if you have not earned it."

"I'll take that as a challenge then," said the high patriarch, chuckling.

"You would be wise to do so," remarked King Raden without smiling.

Merrick glanced around and breathed a deep sigh. "I remember the last time I was here," he said, changing the subject.

"Yes," commented Raden. "You were the troublesome beach brat who accompanied your father."

Merrick laughed, remembering he had gotten into some trouble with the spectar-cart racing. "And you were the serious-looking one always standing at your father's shoulder."

"I hope you won't be as much trouble this visit," the king said, smiling slyly.

"My father trained me well," Merrick said.

"As did mine," Raden remarked.

Merrick quickly changed the subject again. "So, when can we begin the trade negotiations, Your Majesty?"

"The talks will begin the day after tomorrow when the sun is at its zenith," the king stated.

"Why the delay?" questioned the high patriarch.

"This is my kingdom," Raden said pointedly. "You have come a long way. Rest and enjoy the pleasures of the islands. I will decide what is best here. There is no need to spend all your time conducting business."

Krystin's servant, Cemers'ed, showed the king's guests to the Manor House. It was a large mansion with many luxurious rooms. In one room, a long dining table held a dozen platters of fruits, meats, and exotic foods Krystin had never seen before. Merrick's party ate as they discussed the upcoming talks, and then retired for the evening.

In the morning, Cemers'ed awoke them with instructions from the king. He had arranged for an escort to show them the island's wonders that day. As breakfast was brought in, Merrick sighed and sank into a woven reed chair. "I had hoped to begin the talks right away, but I can see Raden will not be rushed."

"Well, I'm excited to see the sights," his wife remarked. "It might be good for you to take some time to relax while we are here."

"I liked coming here better when I was a boy with no responsibilities," Merrick huffed.

"The king seems quite charming," Nizza spoke up.

"Oh, yes, he's charming as a snake," her brother threw back. "A poisonous snake."

"But surely you can charm this snake!" Krystin said encouragingly.

"I'm not so sure. Though he's certainly charmed with you!"

Krystin blushed. "Merrick!" she cried. "It's hard enough for me to get over what happened on the ship. I don't need anything else making me edgy."

"Well, I may need your help in the talks with Raden, so be ready to turn on that smile of yours!"

"All right," conceded Krystin. "I'll help if I can. But I hate the way he looks at me like I'm some shiny, new bauble he wants to add to his treasury."

"I wish he'd look at me like that," Nizza said quietly.

"Nizza!" the couple said together.

CHAPTER 21

I n the en'Edlia palace nursery, Boolie sat stitching on a new playsuit for one of the twins. She loved making these little outfits. They could be done quickly and easily. It was her birth-gift to create clothing, and as the clothier for the ruling family, she was kept quite busy. Her hand could fly across the fabric, adding lace or ruffles in moments. A change of color was equally easy. In her hands, the fabric was like soft clay until she was satisfied, then it became solid and ready to wear.

Now she was crafting a yellow playsuit for red-haired Phyre. Boolie put a muffyberry-shaped pocket on the front. She added a small ruffle over the shoulder straps and it was finished. She would make one in green for dark-haired Jewl.

Leesel sat on the other side of the room casually watching the twins play on the floor with their toys. It was her birth-gift to sense desires of the heart, and the difference between spoken truth and lies. She could sense Phyre's desire for her mother's return. Jewl seemed to be more content, except she was hungry. Leesel smiled to herself. Murm should be along anytime now with lunch.

Boolie finished the second outfit quickly and held them up for the tots to see. "What do you think, girls?" she asked them. "Would you like to wear them after lunch and go play in the gardens?"

Both girls got up from their toys and walked over to see the new outfits. "Mine!" said Phyre grabbing the green one.

"Oh, no, sweet one, the yellow is for you!" remarked Boolie, gently pulling the green one from Phyre's hands.

"I want green!" she cried, as Jewl looked on quietly.

"Oh, but the yellow will look so pretty with your hair, my little muffyberry!" consoled Boolie.

Leesel shook her head. "Why don't you just let her have the green one, Bool?" she asked. "It isn't that important, is it?"

"It was what I pictured when I started," replied Boolie.

Jewl was still watching as she laid her hand on Boolie's arm. "I want green!" cried Phyre again.

Jewl touched the green playsuit which was meant for her. She saw the tears which had started in her sister's eyes. Jewl touched the yellow playsuit which Boolie was holding out to Phyre, who was pushing it away.

Suddenly, Phyre clapped her hands with delight. "Green!" the twin squealed.

Leesel sighed, looking up. "There! Now both are green and the girls don't have to be different."

Boolie looked confused and shocked. "But . . . but . . ."

"I like green!" said Phyre, smiling now.

"Their parents don't mind if they dress alike," Leesel went on. "You know that."

"But . . . but I didn't . . ." Boolie stammered.

"Of course you knew that, Bool," laughed Leesel.

"No, Lees," she finally gasped. "I didn't change the color!"

Leesel grew serious. "What? Of course you did, Bool, I . . ." Leesel stopped midsentence. She could sense the truth in what Boolie was saying. "Well if you didn't, then how did it happen? Who else could have . . . . ?"

At the same time both maids looked down at the twins as the same thought occurred to them.

"Could it be they are showing signs of birth-gift?" said Leesel excitedly.

"I hope so!" cried Boolie. "It would sure help things around here."

"But which one of them did this?" questioned Leesel.

"I don't know. How can we possibly tell?"

They watched the twins intently as Phyre pulled on the now green playsuit and stuck her hand in the pocket. Jewl smiled at her sister.

"Bird!" cried out Phyre, pointing to the pocket. "Bird!"

Boolie laughed. "No, child, that's a muffyberry, not a bird."

"Bird!" Phyre's voice went higher with her frustration as she pointed at the pocket.

Jewl's hand slipped down Boolie's arm and into her hand. She jumped up and down. "Bird!" she cried too. "Bird for Phyre!"

Boolie shook her head. "Why do I even waste time designing things for these girls!" she sighed. "They just want to redesign them anyway!"

Leesel laughed. "Don't you remember Nizza when she was younger, always wanting a different fabric or color or this change or that?"

Jewl reached out, touching the pocket of Phyre's dress as her sister pointed at it and continued to say "Bird!"

"No sense in fighting it, I guess," shrugged Boolie as she took the playsuit in her hand to make the change. Again she gasped. "Will you look at this!"

"Don't tell me," said Leesel, noticing the pocket now looking like a bright-orange Irth Star. "You didn't do that either."

Boolie shook her head. "These girls are showing signs!

Just then Murm opened the door and came in with a tray full of hot food for lunch. Jewl was instantly moving toward the food. "I hungry!" She followed Murm to the table and climbed into her chair. The other maids joined them bringing Phyre by the hand.

Murm passed out the plates and eating ware while the other maids wrestled the twins into bibs. She set out steaming bowls of mozer and vegetable soup with fresh muffybread on the side. Cups of sweetwater and a bowl of fresh, carefully peeled ichy fruit rounded out the meal.

Jewl bit anxiously into the bread. After several bites, she tried the soup. "HOT!" she yelled, dropping her spoon. "Hot!" she said again.

Murm patted her arm. "Sorry, Jewl," she said. "Let me cool it down for you." Murm's birth-gift was cooking and making food just the right temperature for perfect doneness. As one of the many palace cooks she took great pride in her work.

"There now!" she told Jewl. "That should be just right for you."

"Just right!" repeated Jewl, smiling as she picked up her spoon. Then she looked at her sister's steaming soup bowl. "Hot, Phyre!" she told her. "Hot!"

Murm placed a hand on Jewl's arm. "She's so smart!"

Jewl banged Phyre's bowl with her spoon. "Just right!" she cried.

Murm giggled. "Better cool that one down too."

Leesel was sitting right next to Phyre and had seen the steam suddenly cease rising over Phyre's bowl. "I don't think you need to, Murm," she said slowly. "But let me check." She stuck her little finger into Phyre's soup and withdrew it quickly, startled.

"Still too hot?" asked Murm.

"No, it is practically freezing! What happened, Murm?"

"I don't know. It was hot when I brought it in and I didn't do anything to change her soup."

Boolie suddenly stood up. "It was the girls again!" she nearly shouted.

"What?" exclaimed Murm.

Leesel and Boolie quickly told Murm about the changes in the playsuits earlier. "Well I'll be a forkfish!" Murm said in a low voice when they had finished. "So what do you think the birth-gifts could be?"

"Well, it could be changing things to suit their fancy," commented Boolie.

"We're not sure if it's one of them or both," added Leesel.

"Won't this be a grand revelation for their parents!" sighed Murm, then she jumped up too. "We have to tell the high matriarch!"

"I'll go!" stated Leesel decisively. She was halfway out the door before the others could object.

CHAPTER 22

The tour of Raden Island took all day, but it was wonderful. The visitors walked along white, sandy beaches strewn with shells of all shapes and colors. Krystin began collecting them until she couldn't hold any more in her hands. Cemers'ed had accompanied them, seeing to Krystin's every need. Now the servant brought her a basket for the shells. Krystin thanked her, trying to engage her in conversation. Cemers'ed seemed shy and withdrawn as she glanced around nervously, so Krystin just smiled at her.

They rode in one of the king's spectar-cat carts along lush jungle paths. Vines and huge flowers draped the foliage like sparkling jewelry. Strange birds called from above them and animals swung, hung, chittered and climbed through every level of the jungle before them.

They stopped for a rest and refreshment at a spectacular waterfall which plunged from a dizzying height off a sheer cliff into a blue-green pool. The pool water was so clear every rock in the bottom was visible. The spray from the falls cooled the air.

Krystin, cushioned on a lush, green carpet of moss, nibbled on a chunk of palm-bomb fruit. "Oh, Merrick, this is a paradise!" she whispered, not wanting to disturb the enchantment she was feeling.

"I told you," he responded, grinning. "Shall we give up the realm and stay here forever?"

Nizza sat at the edge of the pool, dangling her feet in the cool water. Krystin glanced at her then back at Merrick.

"You're not serious, are you?" she asked quietly, moving closer to her husband.

The high patriarch sighed as he took in his surroundings. He loved this carefree life, peaceful environment and natural beauty. He looked at his wife's smiling face, sighing again. It would be so easy to just turn his back on all the pains of governing en'Edlia. His brother, Jarrius, would do just fine in his place. *But, no,* he thought. *I have sworn to follow my father and serve my country with all my heart and strength. It is my duty and I have already accepted it. I can't walk out on it now, no matter how hard it gets or tempted I may feel.*

Aloud, he said to Krystin, "Of course not! But we will definitely have to plan an annual getaway here, I think."

Cemers'ed stood apart from the island guests, and even the other servants. She used her birth-gift to call a small, lime-green island owl, who sat on her shoulder as she stroked its chest. She could see these visiting royals were different than her king. They were warm and friendly to everyone, even the servants. The high patriarch and his wife seemed genuine in their happiness and love for each other. How she wished she could be away from these islands. She wondered if they would be willing to take her away from here. She would willingly be their slave. But how could she escape the eyes of King Raden? Perhaps during this time away from the king's city she might dare to speak freely to the crown matriarch. Perhaps.

Cemers'ed felt the eyes of the other servants upon her. She dropped her head. *Perhaps not,* she thought despairingly. She sent the small owl fluttering away, as she moved to join the other servants as was proper in the care of the guests.

That evening, after a cooling bath and a change of clothes, Krystin excused herself and went to bed. Merrick and Nizza sat up talking a while longer.

"Merrick, do you think I'm pretty?"

"Of course," her brother replied, not really paying attention.

"You're just saying that because you're my brother."

He sat up then and looked into her face for several moments, while Nizza blushed and looked down, feeling suddenly uncomfortable.

"Well," her brother finally began, "If I were younger and looking for a pretty girl, I would definitely notice your hair."

"Why? Because it's red?" Nizza threw back defensively. She had always felt she stuck out as the only redhead in the family, until Phyre was born.

"No, because it's so shiny and catches the sunlight," Merrick said charmingly.

"Oh" Nizza blushed at his compliment.

"And," he continued, "I would notice how confidently you hold yourself. You are bold and daring. I like that in a woman." He smiled warmly.

"Oh, Merrick, do you think anyone else will ever notice?"

"Of course! But be careful!"

"Why?" asked Nizza.

"Because there will be some whose attentions you may not want."

"Oh," she replied. "I guess you're right."

The next day, as the sun was nearing its peak, Cemers'ed arrived to escort them to King Raden's throne room for the beginning of the trade talks.

As promised there was a sumptuous feast laid out over several long tables. Fruits and edible flowers, sweet, spicy meats, specially prepared grains, and vegetables were spread before them. The meal lasted more than an hour with King Raden dominating the conversation, as servants continued to offer more and more food to the island guests.

Finally Krystin begged permission to stop eating and begin the talks as she couldn't manage another bite. She smiled pitifully at the king. He laughed at her discomfort, but had the food moved away and sent for his scribe.

"Before we begin," the king announced, standing before them. "The women will be removed to another room of entertainment so we men can talk of serious things."

Nizza's mouth fell open, a small cry of outrage escaped her lips. Krystin looked shocked, while Merrick's eyebrows crashed together in disapproval.

"In my country, the women share in the rule of the people and the decisions which are made for all," stated Merrick.

"We are in my country now," replied Raden Rex VIII, "and we will do things my way."

Merrick was silent for several moments as he weighed the situation. He hadn't traveled all this way to have the talks end before they even started.

"Very well," he conceded. "The women may leave, but I shall want to confer with them before any agreements are made. I consider them my counselors in this matter."

"If that is your wish, so be it," announced the king, waving off the comment. "But I find it a sign of weakness you trust your own decisions so little."

Nizza huffed again, but Merrick shook his head at her. Some servants came to escort her and Krystin out as she scowled fiercely at her brother.

"Very well, then. Let us begin," Merrick spoke up as the women left the room. "The day grows late."

*　　*　　*

The crown matriarch and her sister-in-law were led by Cemers'ed away through many doors and past many rooms into another place in the king's estate. When the servant finally turned to them and motioned them to enter one room, they found themselves in an immense room filled with bouquets of flowers, trickling water fountains and ceiling to floor shelves filled with books.

They invited Cemers'ed to stay awhile with them, but her face paled as she looked over her shoulder briefly. "May I ask one question, Matriarch?" she whispered, bowing to Krystin.

"Yes, of course."

"Do the women in your country really rule as much as the men?"

"Yes. There can be men and women on the high council and a woman can rule as high matriarch if her husband dies and there is no male heir."

"I would like to live there," Cemers'ed whispered, bowing nervously.

"Cemers'ed," Nizza began. "How did you come to be a servant of King Raden?"

"It is not my place to say," she said looking down sadly.

"But we are asking you to tell us," Krystin encouraged her.

"I dare not, good matriarchs."

"Please," begged Nizza. "What else have we to do?"

There were voices in the hall outside the door. Cemers'ed jumped. "I must go!" she cried, her face showing great fear.

So she left them alone with a golden bell if they needed anything. As soon as she closed the door, Nizza was exploring the room, while Krystin sat wishing she hadn't eaten so much and wondering about Cemers'ed.

Nizza almost forgot her resentment at being dismissed by the king as she marveled at Raden Rex's expansive library. "Look at this, Krystin!" she gasped. "The Animals of Irth!" she cried as she carefully leafed through the brightly colored, hand-painted pictures. "This must have cost a fortune to have made! How I'd love to have a book like this." She lovingly touched a painting of a crouching spectar-cat in the jungle.

"Couldn't we have a room like this made at the palace in en'Edlia?" asked Krystin, getting up and joining Nizza. "We have a library, but this! This is amazing. I know Tesh could handle the flowers."

"That's a great idea. We'll have to have mother's permission."

"Of course. But just think of it, Nizza!" The two of them were caught up in discussing the creation of a new library for quite a while as they continued to explore the room.

When they heard the door open, they turned expecting to see a servant girl. The sisters were surprised when a blindfolded man stumbled into the room followed by a well-armed guard, who had apparently shoved the man from behind.

The man had bronze skin and nearly white hair which was cut very short. He hung his head, standing there silently, his hands clasped at his back. It was difficult to tell his age as his movements made him seem older than he looked. He was well dressed in a white linen tunic, embroidered with red birds at the hems and neck.

The sisters stood expectantly, waiting for some explanation. Finally the guard announced, "This is Pynottish. By order of King Raden Rex VIII, he will speak to you and you will allow him to perform a 'seeing.'"

"A 'seeing'?" questioned Nizza. "What is that?"

The guard answered, "Pynottish will explain. Now, sit and be silent."

"As a member of the high patriarchal family, I am not accustomed to being ordered around by a mere guard!" Nizza's temper flared.

"Are we to be treated like prisoners?" cried Krystin.

The guard moved to speak again, but the man raised his hand and the guard stepped back.

"Your Highnesses, please," Pynottish began quietly. "I mean you no harm."

"Then what is all this about?" Krystin stepped toward him, gaining courage.

"Please, be seated and I will explain." The man motioned to the guard, who bought up a chair for him.

They all sat, except the guard who retreated to the closed door and posted himself at it as sentry. Pynottish began to speak in a soft, sad voice.

"I am here by order of the king, as Gar has told you," he began. "I am sworn to obey the king. He has ordered me to perform a 'seeing' with the crown matriarch of en'Edlia. Which of you is she?"

The sisters glanced at each other, at the guard, and back at the blindfolded man before them. Krystin finally shrugged and replied, "I am."

Turning his head toward the sound of her voice, Pynottish moved his chair closer to her. He put out his hand. "Please," he said, "I must sit facing you for the 'seeing.'"

Gar came forward and took his hand, guiding him as he scooted his chair toward Krystin's until they sat almost knee to knee. She was not altogether comfortable with this stranger's nearness.

The man sat calmly with his hands in his lap. "When I remove my blindfold, I will look into your eyes and you will look into mine. We will be 'seeing' each other."

"But is that all? Just 'seeing'?" Krystin asked, confused.

"That depends on how deeply you look."

"I don't understand."

"Nor will you until the 'seeing' begins."

Nizza spoke up then. "And what is the point of this, Pynottish? What is your birth-gift?"

The man lowered his head for a moment, then raised it again, answering, "I am forbidden to say. The king has given me a command and I must obey."

Nizza took her sister's arm. "I don't like this at all, Krystin. There is something unsettling about this. Don't do it."

Krystin bit her lip and frowned. "What will happen if you don't obey the king?" she asked the man.

"The king will be angry and my . . . ."

"Keep silent, Pynottish!" thundered the guard. "Just do as you are commanded."

"Please," Pynottish pleaded with Krystin sadly. "I must perform the 'seeing.'"

"What kind of a man is this king?" Krystin cried. "I'm going to speak to him right now!" She stood up and so did Nizza.

Suddenly, Gar advanced on them, drawing a large sword.

"STOP!" shouted Pynottish to them all. "Gar, stand back!" he cried as he unwound the cloth around his eyes.

Gar stepped back to his place by the door, but kept his sword at the ready. The sisters shrank back, unsure what might happen. "Please," Pynottish spoke softly now. "Please, just sit, Your Highnesses."

Krystin sat, but Nizza stubbornly stood at her side, determine to protect her if need be.

Pynottish dropped his blindfold on the floor, and sat silently with his head down, letting his eyes adjust to the sudden brightness. Krystin felt so sorry for this man who must work, it seemed, against his own will. *How could such wickedness be allowed to go on? How could her country consider dealing with such a king as this? How can I help Pynottish?* she thought. She shook her head sadly. *Perhaps there is no way.*

"You may perform the 'seeing,'" Krystin said.

"But Krystin!" cried Nizza. "What if he harms you?"

"Will it hurt, Pynottish?" the crown matriarch asked gently.

"No," replied the man. "You may even find it . . . pleasant."

"Very well then," said Krystin slowly. "For your sake, I will allow it."

Nizza groaned, tightening her grip on Krystin's shoulder, as she reached to take her hand for assurance.

Pynottish raised his head slowly, gazing at Krystin's face. Both sisters gasped as they caught sight of his eyes. He only stared straight ahead into Krystin's eyes.

They were the most beautiful eyes the crown matriarch had ever seen! His eyes were a marvelous pale blue-purple color and full of light. How they shined!

"Oh, my!" Krystin gasped. "Your eyes!"

"Do not speak, Matriarch, only look," Pynottish whispered.

Krystin wanted to look at his eyes. She longed to look at his eyes. She looked deeper.

There were brilliant gold flecks in his eyes like the sun reflecting off the water. How they sparkled. His eyes were ringed with a deep purple, like the evening shadows of a pine forest. His pupils were so black and yet, there was more there. She looked deeper and caught a flash of motion. Intrigued, she stared with more intensity, ever deeper.

Krystin found herself in the pine forests of Lyndell. The sun streamed through the trees casting shadows here and creating glints of gold there. She felt at peace, safe and relaxed. She breathed in the scented air and smiled. It was good to be home, away from the pressures of en'Edlia.

She walked through the trees, thinking of nothing but her joy. Suddenly there was Merrick before her and she smiled. "Let me take you away from all this!" he said taking her hand and pulling her forward.

"But I am happy here," she heard herself say.

"No! You must come with me!" he commanded, suddenly forceful and demanding.

Immediately Krystin felt confused and afraid. She wanted to run away from Merrick. He just wanted to make her suffer. She wouldn't be happy if she left this place. "No!" she cried.

Merrick vanished from before her and she felt her fears disappear. How strange, she thought. She had never feared Merrick after the first day they met.

The scene began to change. All at once she stood at the island falls. How beautiful it was. Again she felt warm and safe.

Again Merrick appeared before her. "You must come with me!" he said, pulling her toward him. Again her fear returned. "No, I am happy here!" she cried and turned to run away with her heart pounding.

Merrick chased after her, calling her name, but with every step Krystin felt her fear of him increase. Then there was another man in front of her. It was a large man who enfolded her in his arms.

He seemed familiar. "Stay with me," he said. "I will keep you safe." She did feel warm and safe in his arms. He made Merrick go away and her fears vanished. "I will care for you," he said to her. "You will have everything you want to be happy."

Krystin felt herself smile. She sighed contentedly. I have found where I belong, she thought, and she closed her eyes.

"You may open your eyes now," Pynottish told Krystin as he replaced his blindfold. Her eyes fluttered open. She was still smiling and had never felt such tranquility.

"What happened?" asked Nizza anxiously. "Are you all right?"

Krystin sighed and looked dreamily at Nizza. "Don't be silly, Nizza! I've never felt better."

"Are you sure?"

"Yes, of course."

Nizza was unconvinced. They had only looked into each other's eyes for mere seconds, yet she was sure something had happened. "What did you do to her?" she questioned Pynottish.

He just hung his head. "I did what I was commanded to do," he replied, standing. He turned to go as Gar came forward and took him by the arm.

"Stay here," the guard ordered the en'Edlian sisters. "The servants will come for you soon." Gar turned and quickly escorted Pynottish out of the room, closing the door behind them.

Nizza looked back at Krystin, who seemed in a daze, still smiling at her. Nizza's concern deepened. She was sure she had seen a tear on Pynottish's face.

CHAPTER 23

From around a corner, Cemers'ed watched as the guard marched Pynottish down the hall to report to the king. Now the great King Raden had found this man who could perform the 'seeing' on Kahn Island in a remote village. Pynottish had been a good man there as he worked on his island with the sick and grieving. His birth-gift allowed him to see into their minds and plant happier thoughts, thoughts which aided in healing of both body and spirit. Raden Rex had taken him from his home and family, and was using him now to twist people's minds to the king's will.

That was how the king had gained his last two wives, and he seemed bent on doing the same a third time. He was becoming extremely bold and greedy to go so far as to try to claim the crown matriarch of en'Edlia!

Cemers'ed had seen this before and she hated it. She was not going to stand by this time and watch it happen to this kind matriarch. She would have to be careful. The right time to reveal the truth would come. *I must warn the matriarch*, she thought. *I must be daring. I must!*

*   *   *

The talks with King Raden had not gone well. Merrick had been frustrated with the king's careless attitude and nonchalant behavior. He was certainly not the serious young man he remembered from years ago.

The king would not be specific about his desires for the trade agreement. The majority of the time he wanted to talk of other matters, continue to eat and be entertained. Many women servants were called in to sing and dance before them. Raden had constantly paraded women in front of the high patriarch, saying men needed to rest after eating. The king had pointed out the beauties and charms of certain servants as served him. He encouraged Merrick to choose one or even two to sit with him for comfort and entertainment.

After more than two hours, nothing of the trade negotiations had been resolved or even briefly discussed. Raden Rex had discussed at length his kingdom's traditions of the king having more than one wife. He talked on, trying to convince the high patriarch of en'Edlia he should adopt a similar policy in his country. He even offered to marry Merrick to any woman from the islands he chose.

Merrick had argued consistently against any such policy beginning in en'Edlia during his rule as high patriarch and his extreme doubt it would ever be adopted by en'Edlia in the future.

"King Raden," Merrick said, standing up and pacing to ease his increasing frustration. "Why is it you have requested this meeting? Why have I come a quarter of the way around Irth to see you?"

Raden sat focused on the latest tray of food which had been brought in. He picked through the fruit slices with indifference, taking a bite of one and then another. As he reached for his golden goblet he looked up as if surprised to see Merrick in the room. "Oh, Patriarch . . . yes . . . what were you saying?"

Merrick's jaw tightened as the vein at his temple pulsed. He clenched his fists at his sides as he stood rigidly trying to control himself. "King Raden, en'Edlia would like to establish trade with your kingdom, but we must decide on the terms and conditions for such trade. That is why I am here. Do you wish to establish this agreement or not?"

The king smiled at Merrick. "Of course, of course!" he said happily. "That is why you are here!"

"Well, then, Your Highness, can we get on with it?" Merrick sighed, returning to his seat opposite Raden at the long table laden with half-eaten food.

"Yes, yes, of course," Raden said waving off another tray of food presented by a servant woman. "Do you see any woman you like?" asked the king, returning to the same subject Merrick had been trying to avoid for two hours. "Just say the word and she will be yours! What about this one? Is she not a beauty?"

"Yes, of course," Merrick replied wearily. "But I am quite happily married and desire no other."

"That is too bad," the king said frowning.

"This is not what I came to bargain for!" said Merrick hotly.

"Don't you have servants?" questioned Raden, ignoring Merrick's comment. "Surely one such as she," he pointed to one of the women, "could serve you well as a servant."

Merrick was insulted at the king's ideas. He was just about to walk out and return to en'Edlia, when Gar, with Pynottish in tow, arrived at the throne room doorway.

A servant ran forward to whisper in the king's ear. Raden's smile widened and he nodded. The servant ran back to Gar and motioned for them to approach the king.

"A moment, High Patriarch, as I converse with my servants," Raden stated to Merrick. The two men stepped before him and bowed. "Well, tell me! Tell me!" the king cried to Pynottish. "And watch your tongue! The High Patriarch of en'Edlia is present as well!"

Gar shoved Pynottish from behind and the man fell to his knees at the king's feet. The fallen man slowly raised his blindfolded face to the king and said, "I have performed the 'seeing', O, King, as you commanded."

"And . . . and?" urged the king.

"I believe it will be as you wished," he finished in a low voice, dropping his head once more.

"Excellent!" replied the king loudly. "You shall be rewarded for your service, as always."

When Pynottish said nothing the guard kicked him. He jumped then muttered, "Thank you, O, King. I am forever in your debt." Gar pulled the man up by the arm and hauled him out of the room.

Raden Rex glanced up at the high patriarch's disgusted look. He smiled again. "You can see he is a man who is faithful to his king," he stated, waving his hand in the air. "It is nothing to concern yourself with."

Merrick did feel concern at the treatment of the strange, blindfolded man. Only the most heinous criminals received such abuse. However, this was not his realm, nor the reason he was here.

"Can we return to the matter of the trade agreement now?" he asked the king again.

Raden, suddenly very serious, gave a quick nod and sent all the servants away. The doors were closed leaving the two leaders alone. It seemed something would finally be accomplished.

"Here are my terms!" Raden Rex said, without hesitation. "I will allow anyone from en'Edlia to visit my kingdom and partake of its bounties and beauties as they wish and can afford. My islands will be the ideal destination for weary workers and landowners needing to, shall we say, get away from it all." He paused, smiling innocently.

"That is most generous, King Raden," replied Merrick, suddenly on guard at the strange change in the king's actions and demeanor.

"I'm not finished!" the king's voice raised slightly. "I will also allow the export of certain of our excess produce four times annually directly to the city of en'Edlia. From there it will be at your own expense to distribute it as you please."

"That is fair," remarked Merrick cautiously. "And in exchange?"

King Raden Rex VIII perched his chin on his fingertips, grinning as he stared intently at Merrick, who felt an involuntary shiver go through him.

"What I want in exchange is a rare jewel from en'Edlia," the king said in a slow, quiet voice.

Merrick still felt something was not quite clear yet. "That can be arranged," he replied hesitantly to Raden. "We have many rare gems in the treasury. Is there something specific you have in mind?"

"Oh, yes," answered Raden slyly. "I have a very specific one in mind."

Again Merrick felt his frustration rising as the king mystifyingly hedged around the point. "Very well, name it!" the high patriarch demanded.

"Its name is . . ." Raden paused for an anxious moment. "Krystin!"

Merrick jumped up from his seat sending it tumbling over backwards. "You can't be serious!" he roared. "Surely you aren't suggesting I just hand over my wife to you? This is outrageous!"

"Calm yourself, High Patriarch," the king commanded forcefully. "Of course that is not what I am suggesting at all," he continued then in a gentler voice. "Please," he motioned for Merrick to right his chair. "Be seated, and let us discuss the matter reasonably."

"Reasonably? How can you even think I will consent to such a thing?" Merrick bellowed still standing.

"Very well, High Patriarch Merrick," the king stated formally. "Here is what I propose. I will not demand nor take your wife by force. However, if she consents to stay with me, then she will be mine and our agreement will be sealed. If she chooses to remain with you and return to en'Edlia, I will still keep my part of the trade agreement in exchange for the right to purchase the desired larger sailing ships we lack as well as other items produced in the country of en'Edlia such as zulijuice, mozers, and muffyberry plants. Do you agree?"

With his thoughts racing, Merrick stalled in giving a reply. He was amazed at the boldness this king displayed. *Just how did he think he was going to steal Krystin away from him?* Suddenly fear seized his heart as he sensed the danger both he and his wife were in. *What had happened to Krystin as he had sat in here for these long hours accomplishing nothing?* The king had obviously manipulated him and perhaps Krystin too.

Merrick's thoughts went back to the blindfolded man. He talked about a 'seeing'. *What was that? Why had the apparent success of that suddenly changed Raden's attitude and tactics?*

Longing to use his birth-gift to probe Raden's mind, Merrick continued to think. He dared not break the global rules of negotiation forbidding any use of birth-gift by either party to sway the talks. That could be a cause for war between their nations and something en'Edlia could not afford right now with all the civil unrest. Yet, had this king, this man, dared to do such a thing, not to him, but to his wife? *How can I find out without revealing my suspicions?* he wondered. *What about Nizza? She might be able to tell me something unless she too has been affected.*

Finally he replied to the king of the Raden Islands. "I must consult with my advisors before I give you my answer."

"That is allowed," responded Raden, grinning again. "But my time is limited and so is yours, High Patriarch," he went on, suddenly in a hurry to conclude the talks. "Since it is my country, I can set the timelines, do you agree?"

"Those are the global rules," Merrick stated flatly.

"Very well, you have until tomorrow morning at tide's turn. Then you and your ship must be ready to sail."

"Agreed," the high patriarch said firmly.

CHAPTER 24

Cemers'ed crept out of the king's estate in the silence of the night. As she moved off toward the Manor House, her thoughts drifted back to her childhood. She had been just twelve when she had caught the king's eye at the annual spectar-cart race. She remembered it well. It made her shiver even now though the night air was warm.

It was known throughout the islands that the king took a new wife as he pleased, which wasn't often, but often enough to have eight now in his fifteen years of reign. He also claimed young women from island families to be his personal servants at the estate. She had been claimed as a servant due him as king.

That day at the races eight years ago, the king had stared at her in a way which turned her blood cold. She clung to her mother beside her in the crowd. As her mother had turned to look, the king had turned away. She had tried to explain her feelings of dread, but her mother had said she was imagining things.

Three years later King Raden had come for her. He arrived unannounced at her humble house of grass thatch and bama pole, with a line of servants bearing glorious gifts for her father in exchange for her. Being poor it was hard to refuse, but her father had done so, as was his right. He wanted more for her than a life of servitude. He loved her so.

Two weeks later there had been a freak accident at her father's work place. He had been nearly killed and left cruelly maimed, unable to work.

Strange, Cemers'ed thought back, *how that had happened.*

The king returned, again offering gifts and pledges of family support for the rest of their lives if they would only give Cemers'ed to him. Again, her father had refused. Three days later her father was dead.

Their home had collapsed, killing her father, while she, her mother, and siblings had been out fetching food and doing daily chores. Cemers'ed knew it had been no accident.

Her mother had grieved her loss for weeks. She knew they could deny the king no longer. Having no means of support and many children to feed, her mother consented, and Cemers'ed was given to the king. Her mother had been supplied everything the family could want. Everything but her brave, loving husband and oldest daughter.

As Cemers'ed remembered her life with her parents, her breath caught in her throat. She felt the old pain squeeze her heart. She covered her mouth and hurried on now toward the Manor House.

A whisper of soft wings and a flash of color drew Cemers'ed's attention to the palm-bomb tree just ahead. There sat her trusted friend, the lime-green island owl she called Faithful. Her birth-gift was to communicate with birds. She had found Faithful abandoned in his nest, hooting mournfully. They had become fast friends and often took walks together in the evening hours. Now Faithful was expectantly peering down at her, eager for her companionship.

"Oh, Faithful! I can't tonight. I have to go to the Manor House."

The owl hooted sadly.

"I'm sorry, my friend. This is important."

Another hoot.

"No, it can't wait until morning. And yes, I will come back as soon as I can."

The owl blinked its large eyes at her, looking sad. "Hoo-hoo!" he called.

"I love you too, Faithful," Cemers'ed replied, smiling. She moved on quickly toward the Manor, her thoughts returning to the king's plotting.

King Raden Rex VIII always got what he wanted. Cemers'ed had seen it happen many times following her own experience. She was determined to stop it this time if she could. She could not help herself, but perhaps she could help someone else.

She spotted the Manor House lights, still on even at this late hour. She was relieved she did not have to wake the good matriarch and her family.

As Cemers'ed approached she could hear raised voices. At her gentle tapping on the woven palm frond door, the room became very still. She tapped again and heard footsteps coming her way.

"What is it, Cemers'ed?" Nizza asked.

Cemers'ed noticed the strain in Nizza's voice, the look of deep concern on her face. "I hope I can help you," she said softly. "May I be allowed to speak to the high patriarch?"

"He is very busy right now. Can you come back in the morning?"

"The morning will be too late. Please! I must speak with him," Cemers'ed pleaded. "It is about the good matriarch and the 'seeing.'"

Nizza's face grew pale at the mention of the 'seeing.' "What about the 'seeing'?"

"Please, let me come in. I am afraid of being discovered," the servant begged, glancing nervously around.

"Very well, but only for a moment. Wait here."

Cemers'ed nodded gratefully and slipped inside. Her thoughts were racing. If she were found here telling them about the 'seeing,' it would mean severe punishment for her and the loss of support for her family. Or worse.

Again, voices were heard from the next room. A disagreement, then silence.

Nizza appeared again, motioning for her to follow.

As she entered the room, Cemers'ed could feel the tension within. The high patriarch stood with his arms folded, a deep frown creased his face. The crown matriarch sat in a chair turned away from him, her back hunched, her face in her hands. Nizza announced Cemers'ed desire to speak. Merrick nodded, but Krystin didn't move to acknowledge her.

"I am deeply sorry to bother you, Your Highnesses, but I come on personal risk with urgent information. Please, may I speak?"

"Very well," Merrick replied.

"As you know, my name is Cemers'ed. I am a servant in the king's estate. I must tell you the king intends to take your wife by trickery through the use of the 'seeing.'"

At these words, Krystin raised her head. "We have already discussed this," she said wearily. "I was not harmed by the 'seeing' in any way."

"Yes, Highness, but the harm will come when you agree to stay with the king instead of returning to en'Edlia with your husband."

"I would never do that!" Krystin nearly shouted as tears filled her already red eyes. "Why would I do such a thing?" she added more quietly.

"Forgive me, Highness!" bowed Cemers'ed. "I do not mean to hurt you, but I have seen this happen before many times. Please, you must believe me."

Merrick stepped forward then to face the servant. "Tell me, how is this done?"

Bowing before the high patriarch, she began to explain. "The 'seeing' is done by command of the king. Pynottish is at his mercy as his family is held here under constant threat to keep him obedient. He must do as the king commands. Pynottish has the gift to plant in the mind of a person some thought or belief which will bend their will to that of the king. I do not know what he has put in the mind of your wife, but I do know that she will, at some sign or word, reject you and cling to the king."

"Is there any way to stop this?" Merrick questioned her with growing panic.

"I have never seen it be any other way than the king's way."

"There must be something we can do!" Nizza said.

"Pynottish would have to perform another 'seeing' to reverse what he has planted, but I know he dare not," stated Cemers'ed. "His fear of the king's wrath is too great." She hung her head sadly. "Your only chance is to leave now. Get away before the king can spring his trap."

There was silence in the room again for several moments, then Merrick spoke. "We thank you, Cemers'ed, for your bravery in coming to us. If we are able to escape Raden's plan, we offer you and your family sanctuary in en'Edlia."

Again the servant bowed. "You are most kind and generous, High Patriarch. I am only a servant and not worthy of your trouble."

"Everyone is of worth and deserves to be well treated," Merrick responded. "I would rescue this Pynottish as well at the risk of incurring the king's anger."

"Oh, please, Merrick, could we?" asked Nizza. "I know Pynottish hates what he is made to do."

"I will do what I can for you and him and your families," Merrick replied. "Watch for one of my men from the ship tomorrow. Go with him. He will know what to do. Now, Cemers'ed, you must go. And thank you. We have much to do before the sun rises."

"You are most kind, great patriarch!" Cemers'ed bowed low before him. "I will be your humble slave forever."

"We will speak more of that tomorrow, should we escape," Merrick replied quietly.

After Nizza let the servant out the back way, she returned to question her brother.

"What are you going to do? How will you trip Raden's trap without getting caught?"

"I have an idea, although I'm not sure it will work," her brother said thoughtfully. "I will need your help, Nizza. It will require both our birth-gifts. Are you up to this, Krystin?"

"Do whatever it takes," moaned his wife. "Just don't leave me here in the coils that snake!"

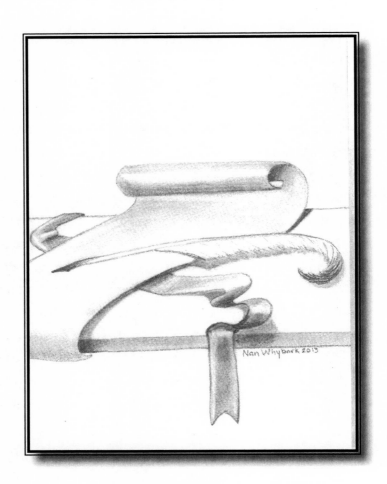

CHAPTER 25

The night had been long, with little time to sleep, but now the small party of guests from en'Edlia stood before King Raden Rex VIII in his throne room. This morning there were no tables filled with food, no women singing or dancing. There was nothing but a small table with the trade agreement documents on it waiting to be signed.

The high patriarch took his time reading the two copies of the document with care, occasionally leaning over to his wife and sister to point out something or make a comment. The king's scribes had written up the trade agreement perfectly. However, Merrick was still painfully uncertain if he would be leaving the Raden Islands with his family intact.

Krystin stood defiantly straight, never taking her eyes off her husband. Inside she was extremely nervous as the time of her test was approaching. She had spent a long time with Merrick probing her mind. He had been exhausted at the lengthy use of his birth-gift, but deemed it critical to their success. Nizza had used her gift as well to calm and comfort them during the stressful ordeal, and then later again to help them sleep.

The high patriarch had successfully discovered the thoughts planted by the 'seeing', but they were strong and he couldn't remove them. He had tried several times to reverse them without success. So after much discussion, another idea was agreed upon which they all hoped would be powerful enough to work.

Merrick was uncertain how the 'seeing' would be used or what would be done to unleash the feelings of fear towards him and trust toward Raden which were embedded in Krystin's subconscious mind. He hoped what he had done, as well as Krystin's strength, would be enough to overcome them. He had warned Nizza not to use her birth-gift once they entered the king's estate.

Now Nizza stared in open distaste at the king, hoping he noticed. She was disgusted as she recalled her initial attraction to him. Her brother had been right all along. He was a snake.

Finally the reading of the trade agreement document was over and the time for the signing had arrived. Merrick picked up the writing instrument, a red-tipped white kahn's feather-quill, and addressed the king.

"King Raden Rex VIII, with these signatures we seal our trade agreement, both sides to be equally bound by it. I have met in good faith, bringing the dignity and integrity of my nation to the table. I must trust you in good faith. I must be true to our agreements. I am willing to do so. I demonstrate this by my signing."

With those words, Merrickobrokt, High Patriarch of en'Edlia, wrote his name with great flourish on both documents. He then handed the quill to Krystin and then Nizza, who each signed both documents as well. Merrick then inclined the quill to the king as an invitation to come forward.

King Raden had been smiling broadly the entire time as he sat on his golden throne. He did not even listen to the high patriarch's speech. His attention lingered on the jewel which would soon be his. He felt confident, even triumphant. *And why not?* he thought. *The 'seeing' was successful. The crown matriarch is as good as mine!*

The king's smile broadened. It had been daring to attempt such a thing. Now, not only would he enjoy the company of such a beauty, but he would also be collecting the very large reward promised him by the Xen's representative he had bargained with a month ago. He would keep the crown matriarch out of en'Edlia forever. The heartbroken high patriarch would be forced to marry another, leaving Krystin's children disinherited and powerless in the realm. He wanted to laugh at his good fortune! How easy it had been to manipulate these en'Edlians.

Now Raden Rex moved to the signing table, casually taking the pen from his opponent. He smiled broadly as he looked into Merrick's serious face. "I am also willing to abide by our agreement," he said, adhering to global traditions. "I demonstrate this by my signing." He scrawled his titled name next to each of the high patriarch's and stood to face him again.

"And now I take my leave of your gracious kingdom, King Raden," Merrick stated coolly, as he rolled up his copy of the trade document. He linked arms with his wife and sister and turned to go.

"Are you forgetting our agreement so soon?" asked the king, still smiling.

"Not at all," Merrick replied. "My wife does not wish to stay."

"Do you mind if I ask her?" questioned Raden innocently.

"Not at all," said the high patriarch, graciously bowing.

Raden stepped closer to Krystin and looked into her eyes. She bravely faced him with a look of defiance. "Stay with me," he cooed to her. "I will keep you safe."

As Raden spoke those words and she looked into his eyes, a kind of peace swept over Krystin like a wave.

Merrick took her hand and she felt a strange stirring of fear as she glanced at her husband beside her. She had never been afraid of Merrick after the first day they had met. Never. This was the trigger! She could feel her fear increasing to near panic. The battle inside her had begun.

She focused on the warmth of Merrick's hand, the memory of their children, the love they shared over the days and years since they had met. Merrick had helped her intensify those memories.

Raden's words coiled around her like a snake trying to strangle her. "I will care for you," he said to her. "You will have everything you want to be happy."

Krystin tightened her grip on Merrick's hand. She closed her eyes as the vision planted in the 'seeing' opened before her. She saw Merrick's face and heard his words, "You must come with me!" he proclaimed.

As she concentrated, Merrick's face faded and was replaced by King Raden. She recoiled from Raden in fear and turned to run. In her mind, she saw another figure, holding out his arms to her. She ran to him and was enclosed in his embrace. As she looked up, momentarily it was the king's face, but it quickly changed to that of her husband. She knew her husband would protect her no matter what. She knew he loved her no matter what. She forced her fear deep inside her and swallowed it like a bitter medicine.

Nothing would come been her and that love. Not hate, not fear, nor threats, or prejudice, or intimidation. The love inside her was her magic. It was strong. She felt it now, giving her strength to resist the fear and the urge to run. She knew those feelings were not real. Only her love was real.

Krystin opened her eyes and looked steadfastly at King Raden as he spoke his words and she waged her silent inner war. Finally, after several tense minutes, she gave her answer to the king.

"O, King Raden, mighty ruler of the Raden Islands," she began, as she released Merrick's hand and stepped toward the expectant king. "I fear many things."

"Yes, yes," he encouraged her, reaching out to take her hand. "I will keep you safe," he repeated. Krystin continued to step toward him, accepting his hand with hers.

Nizza grabbed Merrick's arm, uncertain as to what would happen next.

"I love your islands," Krystin continued. "They are a paradise and I would love to stay."

Raden smiled cruelly, as Nizza gasped in shock. *Victory is mine! I have my jewel!* He wanted to see the look of defeat on

Merrick's face. He longed to see the anguish of loss in his eyes. This was Raden's moment of triumph! Nevertheless, as the king glanced at his opponent's face, Merrick seemed oddly serene, almost confident. *How could that be?* he wondered as he brought his gaze quickly back to Krystin's face.

"But I cannot stay." Krystin smiled sweetly, suddenly plucking her hand away from him and returning to Merrick's side.

Raden was stunned. His mouth dropped open. "What? That . . . is . . . impossible!"

"I will be returning to en'Edlia with my husband. Farewell, King Raden! Perhaps we shall meet again."

"Yes!" cried Nizza loudly. Then she gave Raden Rex a look of disdain and turned away.

Merrick's group was already at the door by the time the king found his voice again. "Wait! This can't be! What magic is this?" he yelled at their backs.

"I'm sure I don't know what you mean," replied Krystin over her shoulder. "You know very well I have no magical powers."

"But the 'seeing' . . ." muttered the king.

Krystin stopped then and turned around to face Raden. "Yes, the 'seeing' with Pynottish, poor man. You really should release him from your service."

"I'll have his head!" Raden swore.

"Oh, I don't think so," Krystin said quietly. She came close to the king then and whispered to him. "Pynottish was very obedient to your command, King Raden, but most unhappy doing so. My husband and I have granted him and his family sanctuary in en'Edlia beginning immediately."

"You . . . he . . . !" Raden sputtered angrily. The high patriarch glanced back as the king regained his control and whispered, "I don't understand this power you have! How could you resist the 'seeing'? Surely magic was involved."

"I keep telling you, I have no magical powers," Krystin spread her hands innocently. "But there is one thing which is more powerful than any magic I have found on either of our worlds. That, I claim as my own magic and source of strength. That is what I used to resist the 'seeing'. And now if you will excuse me." She walked away, leaving King Raden Rex VIII standing momentarily speechless.

Merrick helped his wife and sister into the spectar-carts, while servants were hastily loading their baggage. He hoped his men had been able to carry out his orders earlier that morning.

"Wait!" shouted the king. "What is it? You have to tell me. Come back!" He tried again to enslave her with his words. "You will have everything you want to be happy!"

The patriarchal party waved to Raden, who was still calling out to them and now had begun running toward them. "You're mine! The 'seeing' was a success! You want to stay with me!"

The spectar-carts pulled away toward the pier and their waiting ship as the king came running out of his estate, his face a mask of total disbelief.

As the crew loaded the baggage and passengers on board, Merrick remained on the dock, awaiting the imminent arrival of the king.

Moments later, the king popped up, using his birth-gift to transport himself instantly to the dockside. His face was full of anger and outrage.

"What have you done?" he cried at Merrick. "You have used magic to influence the outcome of our negotiations!"

"Why, King Raden! Such an accusation!" Merrick said calmly. "You know that is against all global rules. Are you saying I should have had to use magic to keep my own wife?"

Raden gulped back his next words, the anger draining from him as he realized he had been caught in his own trap. "I . . . I . . ." he stuttered, as fear crept up inside him. He certainly didn't want a war with the most powerful nation on Irth.

Raden straightened his tunic and cleared his throat nervously. "You are a clever man, High Patriarch," he admitted. "I don't know how you managed it, but you are worthy of my respect."

"You don't know the half of it," Merrick muttered under his breath. Aloud he said, "You flatter me, Raden. But the credit goes to my lovely wife. She has great inner strength and has tamed bigger dragons than you." Merrick smiled broadly. "I recall from our first conversation in this very place, you said respect had to be earned. I'm glad the crown matriarch and I were able to do so."

Merrick bowed, turned on his heel and boarded The Flying Shell. "I look forward to our first trade exchange!" he called, waving the rolled trade agreement in his fist as the ship pulled away from the pier.

The king just stood shaking his head in mystified wonder. "Perhaps I have misjudged women all these years," he mused. "I never imagined a woman could have such strength."

CHAPTER 26

With the Raden Islands out of sight, Krystin began to relax. She strolled on the decks with Nizza and Merrick, once again in her bubble made by Dr. Ikkin. She was glad to be heading home.

Home. She realized she had just thought of en'Edlia as home. That made her smile. She had learned some important things on this voyage. There were things she wanted and needed to remember as eventual high matriarch of en'Edlia.

Merrick left to talk to Captain Acrums while Krystin thought about all that had happened since she had come to Irth.

She had become more confident in herself, and in her ability to show courage and strength when needed. She shuddered as she thought of her encounter with the brash puppet-master, Bafoolee and his efforts to make a fool of her.

Nizza turned toward her. "Are you cold?"

"No," Krystin chuckled. "Just remembering Bafoolee and Kneal."

"Oh, no," replied Nizza. "I'd rather forget that whole day."

"I was thinking about what I learned from that experience."

"That we should always listen to the oracle?" Nizza smiled. "That's what I learned."

"Well, that's a good thing," remarked Krystin. "I learned that not everything can be controlled, especially when there is fear involved. However, I believe fear can be conquered with knowledge, understanding, love, and patience."

"I guess we learned a lot, didn't we," Nizza said thoughtfully.

"As I think about everything which has happened since I came here, it's been amazing and frightening and exciting and scary."

"And what about Manx?" Nizza asked gently.

Krystin squeezed her eyes shut. Her thoughts touched briefly on her encounter with Manx. She quickly pushed the memory away. "I don't even want to think about that."

"You were so brave!" Nizza remarked.

"I was terrified," her sister came back.

"Me, too," Nizza said. "I wonder what fears Merrick has."

"I'm sure he has some," Krystin answered.

"Losing you is certainly one of them," Nizza remarked. The sisters lapsed into silence as they continued to walk toward the bow.

Krystin pondered her experiences. *Had they been useful or just frightening? Had she shown courage or just fear?* Her parents had taught her experiences were always good if you learned something from them.

As they made the turn toward the starboard beam, the sisters passed many sailors working to keep the ship running smoothly. *They must be brave,* though Krystin. *Sailors traveling into the unknown with the weather constantly changing. They must handle whatever happens on each voyage.*

When the sisters reached the aft section Krystin observed the captain, watching over the crew and the ship with careful concern. *He has courage,* realized Krystin as she thought about all the responsibility he had.

Merrick was taking a turn at the wheel as he conversed with the captain. Krystin watched her husband for several minutes as she and Nizza stood by the rail. He had shown great courage many times since they had met. Yet she knew he had felt fear as well.

Krystin thought of Merrick's mother, Narrian, now alone without her husband. She must surely have fears. The high matriarch was a model of courage and fortitude. *Courage,* Krystin finally decided, *does not mean you are without fear. It only means you are willing to act in spite of your fear. Yes, courage is rarely displayed without fear accompanying it. I have a greater respect and understanding for those who show bravery.*

Krystin was brought out of her own thoughts as Pynottish approached, being led by his wife, Stylkra. "The words 'thank you' will never be enough to say how grateful we are to be free of

Raden's control," he began. "Your husband is a good man, Crown Matriarch."

"Yes, he is," she replied smiling.

"And you are a great woman!" Pynottish bowed to her. Krystin blushed at his compliment as he continued. "Now if you are ready, I would like to perform a 'seeing' to undo the cruelty I have done to you."

"Thank you, but I don't think it will be necessary." Krystin laid a hand gently on Pynottish's arm. "You no longer need wear a blindfold, Pynottish," she said gently. "For all who will look into your eyes will find only goodness there."

Krystin watched as he hesitantly reached up, unwinding the cloth from his eyes. His wife shed tears as she looked at her husband's face.

"May the sweet winds of favor ever caress your countenance, good matriarch," Stylkra cried. She plucked up Krystin's hands in her own and kissed them, wetting them with her tears. "You have restored our family and my husband's good name."

The matriarch shed a few tears of her own as she shared the love of the family. Pynottish and Stylkra, heads held high, walked away then, arm in arm, to be with their children in the cabins, as another person shyly approached her.

The young woman with a lime-green island owl perched on her shoulder knelt before Krystin. "I have come to pledge my loyalty to you, Crown Matriarch of en'Edlia, and to serve you forever."

Taking her hands, Krystin raised the young woman up and embraced her. "Cemers'ed, you are free to serve only yourself and your family. I have too many servants already."

"It is too good to be true!" Cemers'ed cried. "My mother and siblings are still trembling in disbelief. We are overcome with joy."

Krystin smiled at the woman who was so close to her own age. "Won't King Raden be surprised at your absence! But don't worry. The high patriarch will see you have the means to get settled once we arrive in en'Edlia." They talked quietly for a few minutes as Krystin stroked Faithful's feathered chest. Then Krystin said, "I hope you will come to visit Nizza and me often."

"Me? Come to the palace?" Cemers'ed covered her smiling mouth. "I could only dream of such things."

"Well, I hope you will make your dreams come true," Krystin replied, smiling back.

The remainder of the voyage was peaceful. The ship made good time with a westerly wind on smooth seas. As the Flying Shell docked in en'Edlia Bay, a large group was eagerly awaiting their arrival, including the entire High Council.

Merrick went immediately to speak to City Council Representative Patriarch Pepperton to make arrangements for the families he had brought from the Raden Islands. With the new families in tow, Pepperton went off to fulfill their needs. Next Merrick spoke to High Keeper of the Peace Degler anxious to hear his report on the capture and imprisonment of the Xen's leader, Bocja. The commander confirmed Bocja was in custody awaiting trial along with several other known Xen members. The rebels had been dispersed, and extra guards were patrolling The Shards for stragglers. Degler also reported Bocja had revealed his treacherous plan with Raden Rex, boasting of its sure success. His confession would seal his fate, Merrick would see to that.

Meanwhile, Krystin ran to hug her children and wept with them in her arms. It seemed she had been gone for a year, when it had only been a few weeks. How close she had come to not returning to them. After several minutes, she felt Merrick join in the embrace. He told her of Degler's report and she nodded in understanding and relief.

Narrian stood quietly among the greeting party until the couple had a few moments to reunite with their children. Then she approached with more good news.

"Some citizen groups have approached the High Council with petitions claiming the crown matriarch does have a magic all her own and they have witnessed it. They want her to be legally made a citizen of Irth."

Krystin's eyes grew wide. "Can it be true?"

Narrian smiled and continued, "What say you, High Patriarch of en'Edlia? Can an off-worlder become one of us?"

"Well, I . . . I . . . ," Merrick stammered in surprise. "I'll have to take it to the council for a vote, but I'm definitely in favor of it!" He drew Krystin closer and kissed her. "Of course, I'm a bit prejudiced." Everyone laughed at that.

Narrian nudged Leesel forward now. Leesel crept up beside Krystin and whispered in her ear. Krystin's mouth dropped open as she turned toward her maid. Soon there was a buzz of questions and responses between her and Merrick and Leesel. Narrian stood by and watched the exchange with a contented smile on her face. She would have much joy in watching her grandchildren grow up.

Then Merrick and Krystin, joined by Narrian and Leesel, took the twins home in the hordle-drawn coach. They were looking at their children with new wonder and fascination.

"Phyre and Jewl are showing signs of birth-gifts!" Leesel had told her.

Krystin suddenly remembered Doogan, the young boy in the market. He had been right after all when he said, "Just wait and it will come." He was right, not only for the twins, but for herself as well. Krystin's heart leaped with excitement. Then she sighed as she thought of what lay ahead of her.

How could she possibly manage her children having magical abilities when she had none? What great challenges would they all face in the future? She thought of the sailors, of Captain Acrums, Cemers'ed and Pynottish.

All at once, Krystin sucked in a quick breath as she felt the movement of new life within her. Sitting so close to her sister, Nizza had felt it too and gave Krystin a questioning look. The others hadn't noticed in the jostling of the coach as they talked excitedly together.

Placing a hand on her belly, Krystin looked at her sister, and Nizza beamed in understanding. With excitement, she pointed to her brother, whispering, "Does he know?"

Smiling, the crown matriarch shook her head. She would tell Merrick soon. Perhaps this time she would give him a son and heir in the ruling family line.

Surely she would need all the courage and strength she could muster for what lay ahead. She looked at Narrian, Leesel, Nizza and Merrick on all sides. She had strength and courage and she was surrounded by others who had them too. She had fears too, but she knew love could conquer those.

Sharing her children's lives would be the greatest adventure yet! She knew what to do. She could captivate them with her own kind of magic. She would love them.

Just love them.

CPSIA information can be obtained at www.ICGtesting.com
Printed in the USA
BVOW070420040313

314572BV00001B/3/P